I0543782

THE STORMBRINGER

ARCHITA MISHRA

Copyright © 2016 by **Archita Mishra**

This is a work of fiction. Names, characters, businesses, places, events and incidents are either products of the author's imagination or used in a fictitious manner. Any resemblance to actual persons, living or dead, or actual events is purely coincidental.

First Printing, 2016
Printed in India

ISBN: 9-78-9383-952-915

Editing: Padmini Smetacek, Wordit CDE
Cover Design: Madan Patil and Avinash Virshid
Illustrations: Sachin Varadkar

 **The Write Place**
A Publishing Initiative by Crossword Bookstores Ltd.
Paradigm, A-Wing, 1st Floor, Mindspace, Link Road,
Malad West, Mumbai 400064, India.

Web: www.TheWritePlace.in
Facebook: TheWritePlace.in
Twitter: @WritePlacePub
Instagram: @WritePlacePub

Printed at: Parksons Graphics Pvt, Ltd, Mumbai

To my parents, without whom I wouldn't have the infinite paths that I do now

EDITOR'S NOTE

IT IS RARE for an editor to be handed, in all seriousness, the manuscript of a novel written by a sixteen-year-old schoolgirl. I opened the manuscript with some trepidation, expecting some childish, half-formed effort. I was in for a shock – a very pleasant one. Archita's writing is surprisingly mature and polished: it is lively and fluid, deceptively effortless. Flashes of wit and humour liven up proceedings at The Manor, refuge of the Invisitae and school for their novices.

As the plot develops gradually, we wait with bated breath, feverishly reading, turning the pages to find out what happens next, always wondering what the untold story is, waiting for the next scrap skilfully handed out in the midst of fast-paced, exciting scenes of action, and before you know it, it's drawing us forward, through loads of vivid description and whirlwind action, to an exciting finish. But no, you shall receive from me no hints to the dénouement!

Besides being Elijah's action-packed journey from a poor farm in the American Midwest to the halls of the powerful Invisitae, this is also, at another level, the story of Elijah's transformation from a child to a young man worthy of the title of *Stormbringer*, of the battle between what he is and what he must become. His powers and his ability to control them are reflected in his own sense of self and his self-belief, and the two sides of the metaphor feed off of each other.

The book and Archita have been a joy to work with and I only hope that you will enjoy the fruits of it in the pages to come. Read on to lose yourself in the world of The Stormbringer . . .

LONDON, 1882

THE DARKNESS OF the night was absolute. Even the moon's ethereal beauty couldn't keep the all-pervading feeling of dread away. Gaslights glittered in their holders, swinging and flickering in the wind. An eerie stillness hung over the London streets, as if the city itself was waiting with bated breath.

A lone figure walked purposefully down the lane, a sense of urgency apparent in his stride. The wind grew restless, tearing at his cloak and hair and causing eddies of leaves to rise up in his wake. It urgently whispered to the man, but the desperate pleas fell on deaf ears. However, the stillness of night can make the boldest man wary, and so he cautiously swept a glance behind him before swiftly ducking into the dark alleyway. He let his eyes adjust to the profound darkness and – after searching the alley – gave a sigh of relief.

He wasn't late.

The silence of the night was interrupted by a startling shriek of wind, and his blood ran cold. It was common sense to not step into dark London alleys, especially at night; you never knew what lurked in them.

This was a terrible idea, he thought. *Why did I ever agree to this?*

He stepped away from the looming shadows and towards the circle of light under the lamp, when the sound of tapping froze him in place. It emanated from the shadows in front of him. He didn't dare breathe as he backed away from the shifting shadows. A humanoid shape materialised in the murky darkness, and took a long stride towards him. Sweat trickled down his neck despite the chilly wind, and he prepared himself to run away from that . . . that thing.

The creature opened its mouth as if to speak, and Fabian caught the gleam of teeth in the darkness.

"Finally here, Fabian?"

Fabian jumped at the deep baritone. It was the sort of voice that radiated power; it didn't have to be loud to be heard. The shriek died in his throat. That voice was as familiar to him as his own. It was the man he had come to meet.

"Eric, you scared me! Don't ever do that again!"

His companion laughed heartily.

"Why are you so on edge? You look like you've had a run-in with death itself!"

The younger man coloured, but said nothing.

"Now, to more serious business . . . You brought the dagger?" Eric asked, his voice betraying eagerness akin to that of a child on its birthday.

"Yes," said his companion, "but I still don't want to go through with it."

"Oh come on, Fabian! Don't start again!" Eric rolled his eyes, exasperated.

Fabian stood up straighter, his indignation emboldening him, and said:

"I just don't understand why you want us to go through with this. You don't even know if this will work!"

Eric's eyes flashed with anger.

"Do you know what it feels like to be doubted for every second of your existence? Mother and Father threatened to disown me because they thought my idea would send me to hell, and that they'd get dragged in with me as well. Don't tell me they've turned you against me as well, after all this time." He stood there, panting, the feral look of a cornered animal gleaming in his eyes.

"How could I, Eric? We're brothers," he stammered.

Eric smiled grimly.

"If only Mother and Father were as honourable as you. I knew you wouldn't let me down."

Fabian swallowed and nodded.

"Let's get on with it, then."

Eric grinned, and Fabian reluctantly returned his enthusiasm. He shivered with excitement as, with an air of finality, they slipped deeper into the night, the shadows shrouding them in a cloak of darkness.

*

Iowa, 10 Years Later:

On the outskirts of the small village of Gordonstown, a lanky boy leaned on his pitchfork and surveyed the wide expanse of earth around him. The ground was parched, full of spider-web cracks that gave him the feeling that it would give way any second. Even the few stubborn weeds that had struggled out from the cracks had been scorched with the heat of the sun. A strong wind blew hot air into the boy's face and gave him little respite from the searing sun. An onlooker, if there was one brave enough to venture into the plains at mid-day, would have marvelled at how the whip of a boy was not blown away by it; he was tall and thin, ribs and spine prominent through his threadbare tunic, a mop of chestnut hair, matted with dust, skimming the collar.

The boy wiped his slender hand across his forehead, though the action was unnecessary; his sweat dried up the second it formed on his tanned skin. He shielded his sapphire eyes from the intense light, and groaned internally. Never in his thirteen years of life had he seen a summer this harsh; the sun had leached out all hint of moisture from the earth, leaving the land dry and barren. His chances of survival were just about the same as those of the trees that had miraculously survived the heat spell: very slim.

The summer had not been kind to the farm that Elijah lived on with his mother. The loamy soil had turned brittle and coarse, and would yield only the toughest of vegetables, if at all. It had become increasingly hard to survive in these less than favourable circumstances. The crops had failed; there was little to eat. Elijah, being a growing boy, got the worst of it. Their family couldn't afford enough food to sate him and his ravenous stomach, leaving him scrawny and weak.

As he thought about this, his stomach emitted the half-hearted growl of an animal that had given up its struggle for survival. Elijah turned to head back to the farm.

A sudden flurry of activity at the corner of his eye caught his attention, and Elijah swivelled towards the sound of the commotion. Anybody who was in the right frame of mind knew that it was foolish to wander into the baking plains. But all he saw was an empty expanse of land. He squinted at the field, and once again saw a flash of colour that was uncharacteristic to the bare, grey land. He blinked, and upon reopening his eyes, he found that there was nothing there.

Convinced that the heat was playing tricks on him, he turned and started to head back, only to be stopped by an inhuman shriek of pain. He spun round and saw the body of a man lying just a few yards away from him. After a heartbeat, he ran towards the still body, his shock disappearing enough for him to regain motor functions. This, he knew, was no figment of his imagination.

The dying man he saw before him was real.

CHAPTER 1

IT HAD BEEN three days since Elijah had carried the ailing man to the hovel he called home, but he showed little sign of recovery. There was a deep gash in his abdomen, shiny with infection, and his forehead burned with fever. His face was purple with healing bruises that he must have obtained from his fall. He lay completely still, almost as if he were lost to the world, but the steady beating of his heart anchored him to his body.

Elijah's mother, Marian, had seen him trudging up towards the house,half-dragging, half-carrying a muscular body that was twice his size, wincing under the strain. His frail arms had threatened to falter soon, so she had rushed out to help. Together, they had carried him into the single bedroom that they owned.

"We can go with a few sleepless nights. What's more important is that we help that man in whichever way possible," she had said to her son, who had only nodded, still in shock.

Day after day Marian tended to his wounds, while Elijah sat there, lost in thought. The man had appeared out of nowhere! There were no footsteps leading to where Elijah had found him, nor any trails of blood. Just the cadaverous man lying in a pool of crimson. He had tried telling his mother, but she had curtly dismissed him.

"Eli, don't make up these fantasies! There is a dying man in our house, and you can't even be serious about that! It's a miracle that he wasn't dead by the time he reached here. God knows where you found him, but it is now our duty to help him. And for the last time: he did not fall from the sky. And if you don't want to be called a madman, you will not repeat this to anyone. Including me."

And so he took her advice and didn't mention it to anyone.

But that didn't stop him from thinking about it.

*

Elijah sat by the man's bed and watched the slow rise and fall of his chest. He pondered over the thoughts that plagued his mind. *Who is this man? Where has he come from? How did he survive such a fatal wound?*

"Eli, sitting around him all day won't cure him any faster! Make yourself useful and do some work that is actually some use," his mother called out from the kitchen, where she was cooking their supper.

Elijah sighed and, with one last glance at the still body on the bed, got up to leave. As he neared the door, a projectile sailed past his head and with a *thunk*, embedded itself deeply in the wood. His wide-eyed glance registered that it was a crudely fashioned dagger. Startled, he turned around, only to be pinned roughly against the wall by a muscular arm. Fighting for breath, he scrabbled at the sinewy limb that had a vice-like grip on his throat, and looked up into the face of his captor. His eyes grew wide with shock as he registered the ferocious green eyes. His captor was the man that his mother had nursed back to health. The one that hadn't so much as twitched since he had first seen him, and had been on the brink of death for just as long. His sudden incredulous joy was quickly drowned by an all-consuming fear. One wrong move and he would be in the man's place. Or worse.

"Where am I? Who sent you to capture me? Tell me!" the man growled. He sounded funny to Elijah, the sounds flowing off his tongue sharper, said with more purpose.

"No one, sir! I don't know what you're talking about! I found you bleeding in the fields and I brought you back to heal. I didn't capture you!" Elijah choked out.

The man glowered at Elijah and smirked snidely at him. "I don't believe you."

Fear-induced adrenaline overtook Elijah, and the boy lunged at his captor. Crying out, he punched the man's healing stab wound. With an anguished shriek, the man fell to his knees, clutching his stomach. Elijah grabbed the dagger from the doorframe and bolted out, slamming the door shut behind him. The man wouldn't stay down for long, and would be back with renewed vengeance. Elijah frantically made his way through the kitchen and ran straight into his mother.

"Do be careful, son! You could have broken a bone or two at that speed." She looked at him and took in his wild-eyed, panicked face. "What is it? You look like you just met with the Grim Reaper! And where in the world did you get a dagger?"

"Mother, we have to leave! The strange man is awake and out for blood!" he said. A tidal wave of panic threatened to overtake him.

"I don't have time for all your games! First you say he appeared out of nowhere and then brand him as a killer? Eli, he's a dead man. He hasn't yet opened his eyes!"

At that very instant, the door that Elijah had just shut was ripped from its hinges and landed in a cloud of dust on the floor. The man stood in the doorway, battered and bruised, but with a murderous gleam in his eye.

"Tell me who sent you, you insolent creature! Did the Occidierum send you?" he yelled, a man possessed.

"Great gods, you were right!" his mother whispered fearfully. "We mean you no harm, sir. I was the one who nursed you back to health." Her voice quavered as he glared at her, snarling.

"Again with that story! When will it sink in?" he growled. "I. Don't. Believe. You."

Elijah blinked, shying away from the man and hiding behind his mother's frame.

"Are you working for the Occidierum?" the man asked, his eyes steely.

"The *what*?"

"Bloody hell, woman. *Answer me.*"

Marian narrowed her eyes despite her fear, throwing the man a glare that would have any sane person run screaming.

"And yet they talk so much about English courtesy," she mocked, having instantly identified the man's accent.

He lunged at the frightened duo, dagger in hand. However, at the last moment, Marian snatched up a metal pan from the table beside her and smacked it into his face with a loud crunch. The man dropped like a stone, unconscious once again.

"There's nothing a good beating can't cure," Elijah's mother, keeping her fear masked, said proudly.

For once, Elijah agreed with her.

The next hour passed in a flurry of activity. They had to remove the man from their home before he woke up with more reason to murder them. Marian, to her credit, did a good job of keeping things under control, especially under the circumstances.

Together, the mother and son carried the man to the dilapidated barn near the house. Years of disrepair were etched into its wooden frame. It was a few strong winds short of falling apart, but it would have to do. The assassin couldn't be kept in their house. The nearly full moon was bright enough to see by, outdoors. But they would need a light in the barn.

"Run and get the lantern, Elijah," ordered his mother, "We have to make sure he hasn't anything else he can attack us with." Elijah obeyed and soon the dim yellow light of a lantern lit up that corner of the barn.

On closer inspection, they found that the man was armed to the teeth: he carried hunting knives in his sleeves, had sharp metallic tacks in his pockets, and even had an ornately carved dagger strapped inside one of his boots. Elijah's eyes were immediately drawn to its luminescence, and he picked it up, entranced

"Whatever is an Englishman going to do with all this paraphernalia? Clean his teeth?" Marian said, gingerly prodding the discarded hunting knives with the toe of her boot.

They dragged from their house another object: a chair. Setting the man down in the chair, they bound him with a chain of steel that was once used for the only cow owned by the family. She had been Elijah's only friend, and he was devastated when she had to be sold off during an extremely rough time. Marian tested his bonds and, giving a satisfied grunt, moved to sit at the opening of the barn, frying pan at the ready.

Elijah sat at his mother's feet, turning the ornate dagger over and over in his palm, careful not to touch the wickedly sharp edges. Its hilt was of gleaming silver, intricately carved, with a sapphire set in it, covered with a scattering of indented stars. The blade of the dagger was made of a crystalline substance that gleamed and shone as it caught the light, so much so that it looked as luminous as the moon itself. The blade was inscribed with the words *vias nostras infinitam*, and Elijah wondered what they meant. However, the unique feature of the dagger that captured his attention was the soft glow that pulsated through it, as if it was a living, breathing creature.

He turned it over again and again, mesmerised by its luminescence. So deeply engrossed was he that he forgot about their captor. A soft groan jarred him out of his stupor. Startled, Elijah cut himself on the edge of the blade. He hissed in pain as globules of ruby-red blood welled up from his cut, and wiped his hand on his tunic before his mother could see. He quickly dropped the dagger to the mud floor.

"Where am I?" the man called out weakly.

"Excellent question. I have one of my own for you: what in the living hell is an Englishman like you doing in the driest part of Iowa?"

He groaned and tried to raise an arm to wipe the sweat from his brow, but realised that he could not; his arms were bound by chains, just like the rest of his body. He closed his eyes, brow furrowing with concentration, and opened them again, looking as if he expected to be in an entirely different place.

"Steel," he said, his eyes growing panicked.

He looked around the barn helplessly for something to free him, his eyes finally landing on Elijah and Marian. The panicked look vanished and became one of anger.

"You," he said, venomously.

Marian gathered her courage and walked forward, the frying pan trembling slightly in her hands.

"Yes, me. And do you remember this?" She swung the pan at him and let it rest just inches away from the man's wincing face. He snarled at her in a desperate attempt to hide his fear, and she tut-tutted.

"You ought to be ashamed of yourself, young man! My son and I devoted all our time and meagre resources to make you well again, and this is how you repay us? By threatening to kill us and snarling like some common beastie?"

He looked taken aback by her sudden outburst. Marian could be frightening when she was angered.

"My son nearly broke his back carrying you to our home, and you thanked him by hurling a kitchen knife at his head!" She picked up the roughly hewn dagger that the man had thrown at Elijah, and brandished it in front of the man's face.

"A dagger," he said, weakly.

"My apologies. *A dagger.* That makes it all better, doesn't it?" she yelled, blazing with fury. The man visibly paled. Elijah cradled his hand and, forgetting his pain for a moment, enjoyed the show.

"If I wanted to kill him, he'd already be dead." The man's bruises began fading and the split skin of his lip began knitting itself together as he spoke. He glanced around the barn, as if searching for something. "Where's the other one?"

"The other what?" Marian echoed, her gaze never moving from his face. Elijah glanced at the dagger, and sidestepped in front of it to shield it from the adults' view.

"The other dagger. The silver one," he said, bewilderment and fear colouring his voice. "You must return it to me. That dagger is not meant for human flesh."

"It definitely isn't, if it's being wielded by a monster like you," Marian spat. She flung down the dagger she held, and the man flinched.

"I meant you no harm, ma'am, honestly," the man stammered, uncomfortable with Marian's scorn. "I thought you were working for someone else."

Marian turned towards her son.

"You see, Eli? The man meant us no harm. He was just inviting us to join his knife-throwing act in the circus. Heaven forbid we thought that he was going to rip our hearts out! Not this gentleman. No, he is much too honourable."

Elijah laughed weakly at the growing expression of discomfort and mortification on their prisoner's face, concealing his throbbing hand behind his back. The pain had spread from his bleeding fingers to his palm. He made sure his mother was still engaged with the task of making the man feel miserable, and brought his hand in front of him. There was a sharp intake of breath as he surveyed the state of his hand. It had swollen up to twice its size and was purpling, as if infected. *Was the dagger poisoned?* he asked himself, silently. As he watched, ropes the colour of tar writhed under his skin, wrapping themselves around his arm. The streams constricted painfully around his arm, and Elijah cried out. His mother and her captor looked his way, startled by his outburst.

"Eli! What on earth did you do?" his mother shrieked, running towards him.

"I don't know how this—"

"Did you cut yourself on the silver dagger? Tell me!" the prisoner cut him off in mid-sentence.

"Yes, but it was hardly a scratch, I swear—" He dropped to his knees, his arm throbbing with a blinding pain. Elijah shrieked, so profound was his agony.

Marian went to pick up the cursed dagger, but the prisoner screamed at her to stop. The fear in his voice made her halt mid-action and she stepped away from the dagger, kicking it to the far end of the barn as she moved.

The man groaned with frustration. Marian thundered towards him and grabbed a fistful of his hair.

"Now don't you dare moan! It was *your dagger!* Do something about it!"

"How can I help when I'm wrapped up like a Christmas present?" he yelled back.

Elijah writhed on the floor, clutching his infected hand and groaning with pain. The black streams had spread till his elbows and continued to move upwards. Desperate, Marian set about removing the man's bonds.

"He's my only son. If you run away without helping him, I'll beat you to a pulp with my frying pan!"

The man rolled his eyes at her, but still looked a little concerned. Once he was out of his bonds, he commanded:

"I need you to leave immediately."

"So that you can escape even more easily? Do you take me for a fool? I wasn't born yesterday!"

He bared his teeth and growled:

"He has begun the Change and, from the looks of it, his body is rejecting it. If you truly want your son to survive, you will do as I say."

Marian gazed at her son, tears welling up in her eyes. She walked towards the exit of the barn. Turning around for one last time, she said:

"If I come back and find my son dead on the floor, you'll have hell to pay."

His expression softened.

"I know," he said to her retreating figure.

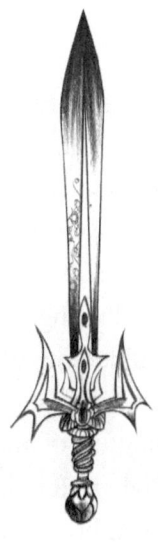

CHAPTER 2

ELIJAH SOBBED UNCONTROLLABLY, unable to contain his tears. He had never felt such anguish before; the pain was excruciating. He could feel the noxious substance coursing through the veins running towards his heart and burning holes in his skin. Vivid explosions of colour burst behind his closed eyelids, blinding him. He couldn't breathe. He gasped for air and doubled over, his body wracked with uncontrollable wheezing. Panic obliterated all thoughts as he desperately gulped lungfuls of air.

"Come on boy, don't fight it! It won't hurt nearly as much if you don't resist it," a disembodied voice said. He found he trusted the serene voice, and let his muscles relax. The voice was right. He was still aware of the foreign streams moving throughout his body, but the pain slowly ebbed away until it was nothing but a slight hindrance.

"Yes, that's it. Now open your eyes and look at me."

Elijah obeyed, and through a film of unshed tears saw a blob which he assumed was a face. His tears rolled away, and he saw the man clearly. He had jet black, unwashed hair and a lean but muscular body. Underneath his grimy, bruised face, he saw high cheekbones and pronounced angular features: all signs that showed that he belonged to a high class of society. His sharp nose was swollen and purple – tell-tale signs of a recent breakage. His striking green eyes had a strange pattern of silver woven into them, just as mesmerising as the dagger itself. The dagger.

"Don't move yet. Your body isn't ready for it. The Change is brutal, but the worst is over. Now we just need to see whether your body accepts it, or not."

His words sounded ominous, but Elijah didn't care. He smiled, his eyes becoming unfocused. The dull throb of his veins was a lulling melody, numbing his senses and making him sleepy. Ah, sleep. It felt as if he hadn't slept in weeks. He closed his eyes again and let himself succumb to the insistent call, only to reopen them when his body was jostled.

"Don't. It makes it easier for the Change to consume you completely. You have to accept the Change, but fight the urge to give in completely. You can't let it get the better of you."

Elijah groaned, his eyes rolling back into his head, only to be shaken back into reality by Fabian.

"You have to stay awake – unconsciousness only makes it easier for it to take you."

Fabian's words sizzled on Elijah's skin as the man said, "*You* control the Change, it doesn't control you."

Elijah snorted in annoyance. This man wasn't letting him sleep!

"Just a short nap . . ." he rasped, his throat suddenly parched.

"No!"

Elijah was about to give a rude reply, but he choked on his words. A gasp escaped him, and his body seized up. The poison had reached his heart. He writhed and shook, his eyes being held forcibly open by the man's fingers. His body started to glow with soft embers of light that gradually grew into a blazing inferno. The heat was intense, and his skin steamed. His eyes glowed, and he shuddered violently. The man drew his hand back hastily to shield his eyes from the blinding light and moved away from the pillar of light that engulfed Elijah.

Just when Elijah thought he could bear no more, the light died down, taking the heat with it. His steaming skin was the only evidence of the flash fire. Both of them sighed, relieved, but for different reasons. A strong arm pulled Elijah into sitting position and made him lean against the barn wall. He groaned at the shift, but was grateful for the end of the ordeal.

"Open your eyes," the man said. Elijah did so. He felt uncomfortable as the man scrutinised his blue eyes with his own green ones. After several seconds, the man sat back, satisfied. Elijah waited for him to deliver the verdict.

"The Change was successful," Fabian said. He smiled sadly. "You're one of us now."

*

The man half-carried and half-dragged Elijah towards the house, wincing as his wounds throbbed with every single step. Elijah passed in and out of consciousness, his gaze unfocused. If it hadn't been for his companion, he would have tripped and broken his neck several times.

The man looked around his unfamiliar surroundings: the dry cracked earth with clumps of sun-scorched grass here and there, the small barn that was falling apart, and the rough cabin that leaned dangerously to one side, made of grey, weathered planks. Using his free hand, the man opened the door to the house. He looked around uncertainly. He didn't know the layout of the house, or where the boy's mother was. Suddenly, the sound of quiet sobs reached his ears and he decided to follow them.

It wasn't difficult to find the mother, the house being as small as it was. She sat in a rickety chair in the kitchen with her head in her hands, body convulsing with sobs. Fabian shuffled his feet and cleared his throat uncomfortably, and she looked up.

"Elijah!" she cried, wiping her tear-stained cheeks and rushing to hug the boy. "Oh, I thought I'd lost you!" Elijah just grunted and slumped onto his mother.

Together, they carried the boy to the room that he had just recently vacated. The door still lay on the floor of sagging boards. He looked down at the dagger, tucked in his waistband, cursing it under his breath. It was nothing but trouble. Now he'd have to explain to the boy who – or, to be more precise, what – he was exactly.

They set him gently on the bed, where he fell into a deep, well-deserved sleep. The Change could be taxing, and he had handled the aftermath better than most. His mother, however, was on the verge of tears again.

"Elijah is all I have left. His father died when he was just a babe. If I lost my Eli, I'd—I'd—" she struggled for words, her bottom lip quivering. The man understood her grief; he had experienced something similar.

"I lost my older brother too. He was only twenty-two when he died. I understand what you feel. I almost lost my senses. But I found a way to cope, and so would you. With your pan-swinging arm, I feel like you can take on just about anything." He smirked and winced theatrically. She gave him a watery smile.

"Thank you, Mister . . . uh . . ."

"Fabian," he said, "just Fabian."

CHAPTER 3

ELIJAH AWOKE WITH a dull ache in his temples.He recognised the scratchy material of the straw-filled mattress against his skin, but he had no idea how he had managed to get here. The last he remembered, he'd been sitting in the barn as his mother interrogated that murderer. His heart spasmed: what if the man had harmed his mother while he had slumbered? But the soft sound of Marian's lilting voice wafted into the room from the kitchen and Elijah sighed audibly.

Elijah wracked his brain to wade through his hazy memories, but he drew a blank. He remembered a few details – a blinding light, heat to scorch his eyelids, and immeasurable pain. Whatever else he'd managed to forget, he remembered the pain full and well.

Remnants of the pain still lingered in his person. His eyes felt like they'd been stung by nettles, and his tongue felt dry and leaden in his mouth. He yawned, unfathomably tired, but the movement strained the weary muscles in his chest. He swung his legs over the side of the straw bed, groaning at the effort, and pushed himself into sitting position. Immediately, the sparsely furnished room swam around him and Elijah felt the urge to throw up. He took deep breaths to steady himself.

"How did I get here?" he wondered aloud.

He got up from the bed and stretched to relax his tense muscles and stiff joints. The dull throbbing of his head had ceased. He made his way to the tiny bowl in the corner of the room that served as a washbasin, and splashed his face.

The contrast of the cool water against his skin after the intense heat was deliciously welcome, and Elijah shivered at the sensation. He washed the grime from his face and looked at his reflection in the mirror, only to jump back in surprise. Something was amiss.

He scrutinised his features in the mirror with calculative precision. He noted the bones jutting out at sharp angles and the smooth pale skin stretched tightly over them, familiar products of months of empty bellies and rationed meals. Elijah brushed the dark hair that flopped into his eyes, making a mental note to request Marian to shear it for him. Elijah turned back to the mirror and jumped back, his eyes narrowed suspiciously. He brought his face close enough to the mirror for his breath to mist the glass and stared into his eyes, realising why his face seemed so different. His azure irises glowed with intricate patterns of silver, giving them an ethereal quality. He looked at them from several different angles, hoping it was a trick of the light, but the patterns laced into his eyes didn't diminish.

Suddenly the memories from the past few hours crashed into Elijah, and the boy swayed under the onslaught of information. He remembered cutting himself on the dagger, remembered the agony of writhing around on the barn floor, remembered the face of a man looming over him as he convulsed, his voice a soothing balm to Elijah's panic. With a start he realised that the man had silver flecks in his emerald eyes, almost identical to the ones that now graced Elijah's irises. He must know what had happened to Elijah. He had to.

Belatedly, he also realised that the man had been armed, and had earlier tried to gut him like a pig. But Elijah had to know what exactly had happened to him, and the man was as good a place as any to start seeking answers. Elijah breathed deeply, steeling himself as he looked into the mirror. He had no choice.

He had to confront the man who had tried to kill him.

*

Elijah tiptoed towards the kitchen, keeping close to the walls to ensure the man wouldn't catch him unawares from behind. He had a short distance to cross, but he began panting with exertion. The door was back in place, and ajar.

He peeped round it and saw his mother gesticulating energetically as she stirred the contents of a pot and simultaneously talked to the man, who was sitting comfortably in a rickety chair.

"What will happen, Fabian? He's just a child! He can't just *leave*! What will I do without him? Besides, he can't handle the outside world, and the training that you mentioned sounds too gruelling for Eli," Marian said, stirring the contents of the boiling pot furiously to mask her growing concern. The smell of a substantial stew wafted towards Elijah, tantalising his taste buds. His mother hadn't prepared such a rich broth in a long time. He cocked his head at the heady, meaty scent of the stew and wondered where she had got the ingredients. The closest marketplace was two villages away and, irrespective of the location, the family had no money to spend on meat. Nevertheless, his stomach gurgled hungrily.

"Marian, he has no choice. The Brotherhood is the best option for him now. If the Occidierum find him, there's no saying what they'll do! They've hunted us for *centuries*, Marion. Trust me, this is his best chance."

"My best chance for what?" Elijah asked, walking in and curiously glancing between his mother and the killer whom his mother had casually referred to as Fabian.

"Eli! You're awake." His mother ran to him and gathered him in her arms, hugging him fiercely. "I thought I'd lost you forever. You've been out cold for a whole day!" she said, her voice shaking with emotion.

He irritably pried her arms off him.

"But you didn't," he snapped. "My best chance for *what?*" he asked again, addressing Fabian, who was taking a sudden interest in the wooden table. He felt his mother shift uncomfortably beside him.

"Now, Eli. This gentleman has been ever so kind and supplied us with the ingredients for our meal. Supper is almost ready, let me just—"

"*Answer me!*" Elijah yelled, the veins in his neck bulging with anger. His mother jumped back startled, and Fabian flinched.

He looked up from the table and with exaggerated slowness said:

"For your survival."

The sentence hung in the air. It reverberated in Elijah's ears and caused his head to spin. The words sounded more ridiculous every time he thought of them. He laughed, trying to diffuse the tension and said:

"I am a farmer's boy. I have never set foot outside this village and have seldom met anybody other than my mother and the occasional straggler. Who would want to kill me?"

The man shook his head, smiling balefully to himself.

"The real question is," he said, "who *doesn't* want to."

Fabian's words left an almost audible hum in the room, the tension behind them almost palpable. Elijah didn't know how to react or what to say. He stood there, slack-jawed, as his mother and Fabian looked at him, concerned.

He sank to his knees and placed his head in his hands, snorting derisively.

"What is it, son?" his mother asked, clearly troubled by his reaction.

"This is utter nonsense! A week ago, the only potential threat to my life was the drought, and suddenly that becomes the least of my worries!" he said, looking up. "How do I know that I can trust you? After all, you *did* try to kill me," he said pointedly, addressing Fabian. The man turned scarlet at the memory and cleared his throat.

"Because he's like you," Marian whispered uncomfortably.

"Like me?" Elijah said, confused.

"I think it's time we had a talk, don't you?" Fabian said, rising. "Come outside with me and I'll answer all your questions."

*

"I'm a what?" Elijah asked again.

"An Invisitus," Fabian said for the tenth time. He was being uncharacteristically patient with the boy, ignoring his annoying habit of repeating himself.

"And what is that, exactly?"

He suppressed a sigh and replied:

"Invisitus. It literally means 'surreal'. The things we can do are, to put it quite simply, unbelievable."

He sensed another question and held up his hand for silence.

"We, Elijah, have the ability to travel wherever we want to. We can teleport across oceans, or even just a few small steps, before you can say 'vanish!' – and much more." He stopped himself from throwing his hands up in irritation as the boy narrowed his eyes suspiciously.

"It all depends on how much experience and practice you have. Which is why I'm trying to convince you to come with me."

"Everything that you're saying is *completely* outrageous! How can I be sure that you're speaking the truth? I have no proof and I'm sure you'll agree when I say that our first encounter was rather . . . troubled."

Fabian ground his teeth with anger.

"You want proof? Fine, I'll give you proof!"

He took a few steps before turning to give Elijah one last glare over his shoulder, and vanished. Elijah jumped back, scanning the land for any traces of the man. After squinting into the far distance, he saw a humanoid figure materialise by the closest farm in the vicinity and saunter towards the setting sun before vanishing again. Elijah stared slack-jawed, whirling expectantly and trying to locate the man.

Someone tapped Elijah on the shoulder, and he shrieked. He swivelled round, face-to-face with Fabian, who was grinning smugly.

"Enough proof, then?"

Still at a loss for words, Elijah nodded.

"Although we have to teach you to harness your powers, your safety is of more importance. If word gets out that you are one of us, your mother's and your life will be jeopardised. There is no telling what they might do."

"They?"

"The Occidierum. They are none of your concern. At least, not if you decide to join me. The Brotherhood of Invisitae will teach you all you need to know about our life. But remember, whatever choice you make now, your life will never be the same. There's no turning back."

Elijah swallowed. Beads of sweat gathered on his forehead and trickled down his chin. *If I stay, Mother would be in danger. From people I hadn't heard of, before today. But if I go away . . . I could possibly save Mother's life, not to mention mine*, he thought.

And it wouldn't hurt to learn more about these Invisitae, he admitted.

Fabian twitched round nervously, peering anxiously at Elijah.

"Well?"

Elijah looked up gravely.

"I have made my choice."

CHAPTER 4

MARIAN WAS BUSILY packing all of the few belongings that Elijah possessed. She folded and arranged his clothes in a small cloth satchel in a frenzy. *It'll help keep my mind off Elijah,* she thought. This triggered a wave of emotions in her and her eyes brimmed with tears. She blinked them away furiously, determined not to appear weak in front of her son. She lifted up a tattered shirt made of coarse, thick wool not unlike woven rope. *I had made this myself,* she reminisced, *when times were so hard that we couldn't afford cloth.*

She began folding it with a deliberate slowness, smoothing out the wrinkles. She couldn't bear the fact that she'd have nothing to remember him by. He would just be another ghost of her past, haunting her till the end. She clutched the shirt to her chest, the coarse material snagging on the front of her dress. She couldn't get herself to put the rag in the satchel.

"He won't need it anymore. The Invisitae will clothe him and care for him like I never could," she said under her breath. She tucked the shirt into her apron, the comforting coarseness a constant reminder. She wouldn't let Elijah slip from her hands completely.

"Mother?" Elijah asked, hesitant to approach her.

His reluctance to say goodbye was just as profound as his mother's. This was the first time he was leaving her side; how could he survive out there without Marian's vigour?

"I . . . I'm sorry. If I hadn't brought Fabian, then—"

Marian stood up, her eyes glittering. With defiance or tears, Elijah couldn't tell.

"Then he'd be lying dead in the fields. You saved his life, son! *Never* apologise for things that are not under your control, Eli. This was meant to happen." Her bottom lip quivered.

Fabian walked into the room and paused, sensing the intense emotions in the air. He cleared his throat awkwardly.

"Are you ready?" he said.

Elijah opened his mouth, but Marian nodded before he could answer. She handed the satchel to her son, who accepted it with shaky fingers.

"I love you son," she said, her eyes brimming with tears. "Do me proud."

Elijah nodded and bowed his head to hide the tears slipping down his cheeks. She hugged him fiercely, then let him go. Elijah shouldered the satchel and followed Fabian, who had elected to lead the sombre procession towards the front door. He paused inside the threshold, letting Elijah walk out before he turned to Marian.

"Thank you," he smiled, a blush unfurling on his cheeks like the petals of a flower.

Marian responded in kind, saying:

"Protecting my son will be thanks enough."

"With my life," Fabian replied, curling a fist over his shoulder in an oath. The desperation in her words was palpable, and Fabian's heart constricted painfully at the love her words held. Having never fully experienced the extent of a mother's love, it had been a while since he'd witnessed a bond so strong.

Marian watched the figures grow smaller and smaller as they strode towards the horizon, her body sagging against the doorframe. She braced a hand on her chest, and staggered into the kitchen, scrabbling at the shirt concealed under her apron. With shaking fingers, she unfolded the now crumpled shirt, clutching at it like a lifeline. She sat down in a chair and wept now that there was no one to see her tears fall. She wailed with unadulterated anguish, lamenting for a son who would perhaps never return.

*

As the duo trudged over the fields, Fabian flicked his eyes towards the boy: his shoulders were set with grim determination, his hands balled into fists at his side. Despite the stone-cold look on his face, his eyes threatened to drown under another flood of anguished tears. He wanted to say something to comfort him, but doubted that his words would have any positive effect.

Oh well, he thought, *it couldn't hurt to try.*

Fabian cleared his throat and placed a hand on the boy's shoulder. Elijah looked up, startled, as if he had forgotten about his companion. He blinked rapidly, suppressing the tears.

"Elijah, bear up. Once you are fully trained, and able to defend yourself and your mother, you may come back. For now, this is the best thing you can do for her."

Elijah nodded, lips pressed firmly together. Fabian was right. He must move on, for now. His thoughts turned in another direction.

"Fabian, can I ask you something?"

"You just did," he replied with a weak smile. "Go ahead."

"How did you end up here?" Elijah asked.

Fabian froze. The boy's question brought back a torrent of painful memories: a blinding light followed by darkness, a writhing pillar of smoke, and an anguished shriek which resonated in his entire being. The memory was so vivid and clear that it might as well have been happening then and there.

Elijah, who had continued walking, oblivious to Fabian's reaction, noticed his absence for the first time and turned around to look at him. Fabian stood statuesque with his eyes clamped shut, his expression growing more and more troubled every second until he sprang back suddenly, his eyes flying open once again.

"That," Fabian said, taking a deep breath to steady his nerves, "is none of your business."

The duo resumed walking, a stony silence accompanying them.

"That's alright. It was wrong of me to pry," Elijah said to the stony-faced man. "I was just wondering."

It wasn't direct, but it was an apology of sorts, so Fabian decided to let it slide.

"Come, this is the spot," he said.

They had reached the spot where Elijah had first found the dying man so many days ago. Elijah angled his body away from the spot, expecting to see the ground stained red with blood; instead, he saw a small plant with a single flower growing out of it. The flower's large petals were snowy white and the edges of the petals were tinged with scarlet. Elijah stared in wonder.

"*Vitta sanguine*," said Fabian. "Bloodlace. I'm sure you know where it gets its name from."

Elijah nodded slack-jawed, transfixed by its beauty.

"It has restorative properties when used correctly and helps speed up the process of curing wounds on injured Invisitae . . . not that we don't heal well enough on our own, as I'm sure you've noticed."

Elijah watched, mouth hanging open, as Fabian bent down and plucked the delicate stem from the ground. He held it out for Eljah to hold. The boy shied away from it. His experience with the dagger had taught him that not all things beautiful were to be trusted.

"Go on," Fabian urged. "It can't harm you."

Elijah stroked its silky petals and sniffed the flower. He recoiled instantly: the petals bore the sweet, cloying smell of blood. Fabian chuckled and carefully tucked the flower into the pocket of his coat.

"Best be off," he said to Elijah.

"Where to, first?"

"London. I have a score to settle with an old *friend* of mine," Fabian replied and offered his hand to Elijah. "Ready?"

"He isn't one of those dangers you mentioned before, right? He—he won't hurt me, will he?" Elijah stammered.

Fabian's lips thinned.

"Raven is just as notorious as the bird he's named after," he said. "Of course he'll try to hurt you." Fabian looked over at Elijah's blanching face and snorted. "Don't look so scared, boy. You'll soon get used to my sense of humour. "

"Or lack thereof," Elijah muttered, the colour returning to his face. Fabian didn't seem the type to make jokes, even unfunny ones.

Despite himself, Elijah shivered with excitement and gripped Fabian's hand tight. He looked over his shoulder one last time at the life he knew and turned back to face the setting sun.

"I'm ready."

*

A wizened old farmer clawing at the fruitless ground with his rusted mattock stopped his ministrations and leaned on his implement, wiping the sweat off his brow and glaring at the sun that blazed steadily at the lip of the horizon. He saw the silhouettes of two people walking towards the sun, their shadows growing longer and longer as they walked, painting the parched ground in a shroud of black. He was watching the two figures with a keen eye, when suddenly the two mysteriously vanished. He blinked several times, rubbing his eyes disbelievingly. He stood, unmoving for several minutes, before shaking his head.

"First I see mysterious lights, and now vanishing people . . . The heat really *is* driving me mad!" The man grabbed his pitchfork and continued his futile work, barring his mind to the possibilities the world held.

CHAPTER 5

LONDON WAS A land with many faces. To most, the city seemed ordinary: streets bustling with life, gardens full of people with a taste for tranquillity, and markets overflowing with the din created by the haggling of vendors and buyers alike. But, beneath the maze of gas-lit alleyways and cobbled streets, the city hid something unknown and mysterious. Dangerous.

The two landed in one of London's many alleyways, just off a main street. Fabian straightened the skewed collar of his waistcoat and brushed invisible specks of dust off his coat. He started at the sound of a heavy thud and whirled around, coming face to face with his companion lying on the ground on his back. Elijah's face was hidden behind plumes of dust and dirt, his eyes squeezed shut upon impact. He groaned and stood up, wiping the grime from his eyes. Fabian suppressed laughter as the boy grinned at him through the newly acquired layer of filth on his face. He looked dazed, intoxicated with the sensation of leaping across oceans, hills, rivers, cities in but a second.

"I can't . . . I mean, I—I—" the boy stammered, at a loss for words.

Fabian laughed heartily.

"I know what you mean. Now get yourself cleaned up," he said, producing a kerchief from one of his many pockets and handing it to Elijah.

Elijah accepted it gratefully with trembling fingers. He swabbed at the dust on his body, but could do little for the grime coating his hair. Finally giving up, he asked:

"Where are we?"

"In an alley just off Thames Street, near Blackfriars Bridge," Fabian said. After registering the clueless look of the boy he added, "That's in London."

Elijah sniffed the air, and his nose was immediately assaulted with the smell of soot and the murky smell of dirty water. His nose wrinkled in distaste.

"This friend of yours, where do we find him?" he asked.

"I'm not entirely sure . . . he's rather difficult to pin down."

"Are we going to . . . ah, *teleport* to his location?" the boy said, unable to suppress his giddiness at the prospect.

"I'd rather we walk," Fabian replied curtly. "People don't take too kindly to strangers turning up from nowhere, and it is risky to teleport without clearly knowing where you are headed. You might end up embedded in a wall! Besides, you aren't going to meet him. It's simply too dangerous and you aren't experienced enough to handle it again, so soon after the last."

The fire in Elijah's eyes dimmed and his shoulders sagged. He hated being told he wasn't good enough. Fabian looked away from the crestfallen boy. He was in no mood for negotiations.

"Come along now," he said and resumed walking, Elijah following forlornly.

The companions emerged onto the main road and were greeted by an overwhelming onslaught on their senses. The pavements on either side of the road were overflowing with commuters, some clothed in vibrant swathes of silk and adorned with pearls and jewels while others wore second-hand breeches and patched skirts. The blinding sun caused waves of heat to roll off the steaming roads. Several women carried parasols to shield their faces from the incredible heat and light and travelled in twos or threes. Richly embellished horse-drawn carriages and rough carts trundled along the road and weaved their way through pedestrians that crowded around nearby shops. A little way up the road, several carriages were packed together, blocking the road. Seeing this as an opportunity, hawkers and eager flower-sellers dived madly in and out of the throng of carriages, advertising their wares raucously.

The street was filled with refined chattering and guttural shouting, occasionally interrupted by bursts of laughter from people and neighs from the horses. The smell of baking bread wafted into the air and mingled with the putrid scent of rotting garbage. The river Thames glittered in the distance, a majestic bridge stretching from one bank to the other like a granite cat. The bridge teemed with pedestrians that looked like china figurines from such a great distance.

"Blackfriars Bridge," said Fabian.

Elijah whirled around in awe, drinking in the alien sights and smells. He had never seen so many people gathered in one place. He ran to a nearby shop that sold sweetmeats and inhaled the smell of fresh sugar, his eyes drifting closed with pleasure. He looked around at shops advertising *The Finest Leather in all of England* and *The Newest Fashions around the World* with an expression of growing wonder. He had never seen a place more heavenly.

"Come on, boy! We haven't got all day!" Fabian said, dragging Elijah away by the arm and jarring him out of his stupor. Elijah followed, looking longingly at a poster for *Fantasmo's Fantastic Circus* hung up by the butcher's.

Fabian followed his gaze and dragged him towards the poster. He looked hard at the sheet which bore a hand-painted picture of a tall, thin man clothed all in black. The man had a thin moustache and a goatee. Coupled with his attire and his fancy top hat, it gave him an air of mystery. Fabian scrutinised the picture and, after several minutes, gave a satisfied grunt. He had found what he wanted.

He turned towards Elijah, who had been closely watching Fabian's every move and asked:

"How do you feel about a visit to the circus this evening?"

*

For Elijah, London was a dream come true. Once the decision to visit the circus had been made, Fabian began looking at more immediate issues: like Elijah's dismal state of dress.

"You can't wander around London looking like a street urchin!" he proclaimed, dragging Elijah to the barbershop.

The barber was a frail, bespectacled old man with little hair himself. However, his skill with scissors surpassed that of Marian's. In fifteen minutes flat, Elijah's hair had been washed and trimmed in a neat and presentable manner. Gone were the days of blowing hair out of his eyes, and Elijah felt his new haircut made him look very distinguished. He could almost pass for a Londoner, had it not been for his clothes.

The shopkeeper at Inglot's Clothing Emporium was tall and stick-thin, with a waxed moustache and a pair of gold-rimmed spectacles balanced on the tip of his aquiline nose. His expression, as he glanced at Elijah's apparel, went from being condescending to that of utter revulsion, his eyebrows nearly disappearing into his receding hairline. He crossed his arms and looked at Fabian gravely. In a voice as slick as his moustache he droned:

"Sir, there is not much I can do to help this . . . boy," he sighed dramatically for effect, "But nevertheless, I will do my best."

Elijah turned scarlet with embarrassment. The insult was implied so subtly that it hurt even more. The shopkeeper motioned for Elijah to follow him into the fitting chamber. He looked at the neatly piled clothes and selected a few garments that were Elijah's size and threw them at the boy. He went to a small cupboard, bent down and pulled out a couple of pairs of sturdy shoes. They joined the little pile of clothes lying before Elijah.

"Try these on. Come on, I haven't got all day, you know!"

Elijah pulled off his clothes and slipped on a light-blue shirt and a pair of brown trousers, which promptly slid right off him.

"You *do* know that you have to secure the trousers with the suspenders provided, I hope."

Elijah grew beet red and pulled up the trousers again, this time securing the suspenders onto them with fumbling fingers. He dragged on a vest and a coat and hastily stuffed his feet into a likely looking pair of shoes. He bent down and fastened them, and stood up. The shopkeeper tut-tutted loudly and shook his head.

"Woe betide me! Never have I met a more, for lack of a better word, simple boy. Tell me, you are from the countryside, are you not?" he addressed Elijah, who nodded with embarrassment. "So, you must be the good sir's charity case. He seems *much* too thoroughbred to be your father."

Elijah balled his hands into fists as the man walked around him, making adjustments to his attire, oblivious to his customer's growing anger.

"My father is no more. I live with my mother," Elijah said through gritted teeth.

"An American. That explains it all, doesn't it?" The man shook his head, as if deeply saddened. "I presume it was your mother that dressed you, hmm?"he said, buttoning up the shirt's collar right up to Elijah's throat.

"Not a very capable mother, is she?" the man said, smirking derisively, "judging by your tattered rags that supposedly pass for clothes. Why, I'll bet my buttons that *shirt* was her handiwork! Only lowlifes from the countryside are capable of creating such horrendous garments." The man snickered as he put the finishing touches to Elijah's clothes.

The boy bared his teeth and snarled:

"My mother did the best she could, and you are nobody to criticise her!"

"Watch it, urchin. I'm not your beloved *mother* to humour you. If you love her so much go back to her and wear her handmade rags and roll around in your own filth, why don't you!" the shopkeeper barked.

Elijah was blinded with a profound anger that washed over him in a flood. He would not have this man insult his mother in front of him. Despite their lack of funding and resources, Marian had done all in her power to provide for him, and Elijah wouldn't let this rodent abuse her efforts.

His body grew uncomfortably warm and pulsated with an eerie glow, and rose a few inches off the ground. The man gave a squeak of surprise and jumped back, crashing into a table and knocking his glasses askew. Elijah's eyes glazed over and turned a solid silver. A gale of wind picked up around his hovering body. Clothes were ripped off their hangers and dragged off shelves. They flew around the room in a whirlwind and pelted the shopkeeper, who sat cowering in a corner, praying incoherently to the heavens.

Suddenly, the door to the fitting room crashed open, revealing an alarmed Fabian. He took in the scene and charged into the room, holding up a hand to shield himself from the harsh wind and torrents of clothes. He made his way towards Elijah and placed his hand on the hovering boy's shoulder.

Elijah turned to face Fabian with impassive silver eyes, irritation flashing across his features, and Fabian recoiled, drawing his hand sharply away from his blazing shoulder. Elijah's skin became uncomfortably hot, and began to itch. The muscles in his face began twitching as his skin crackled with energy. The air between his fingers sizzled and popped.

Fabian's eyes grew wide as the light flickering within Elijah concentrated into his fingertips, shivering and dancing across his fingernails in forked prongs. Fabian's blood ran cold.

"Stop this at once," he cried. "You mustn't give in to your power! *This isn't who we are!*"

Elijah squirmed at the building tension in his forearms, but as soon as he heard the fear in Fabian's voice, the blistering heat subsided. The wind slowly died down, and all the clothes dropped to the ground. Elijah's body stopped glowing, and his eyes returned to their original state. He floated downwards and landed shakily on his feet near Fabian, who steadied him.

"What . . .what happened? Did I do this?" Elijah muttered, looking around.

Fabian looked up, panic flashing across his features.

"We need to leave. *Now*. If they find us here, there's no saying what they'll do . . ."

"Who?"

"Stop asking questions and help me!" Fabian barked.

Fabian's panicked tone worried Elijah, but he did as he was asked. Together, they lifted up the shopkeeper (still mumbling under his breath) and placed him in a chair. He opened his eyes and looked around. When they landed on Elijah, he began shrieking and kicking and flailing in his sheer desperation to escape. Fabian restrained him and forced him to gaze into his eyes.

"Look at me. You won't remember a thing about this encounter. We were never here," he said slowly and authoritatively, glaring into the eyes of the terrified man, who gazed back, afraid. Elijah doubted Fabian's words would make the man forget, but to his amazement, the man nodded and his gaze grew unfocused. In seconds, he had shut his eyes and was snoring away.

Making sure the man was truly asleep, Fabian looked warily at Elijah, who was still glancing worriedly at the dozing figure.

"Come on. We mustn't be found in here," he said, and beckoned Elijah to exit the shop.

Elijah took one last look at the mess he had made and exited, Fabian following closely behind,flinging a gold sovereign in the man's lap as he left. *Things will be more exciting than I thought*, Fabian mused, *but I'm not entirely sure that's a good thing.*

CHAPTER 6

ELIJAH STRODE AWAY from the shop, his hands balled into fists, tears of anger stinging his eyes. The man might have forgotten the incident, but Elijah had no such luck. He remembered *everything*. In that trance-like state, Elijah had felt invulnerable, unstoppable. Powerful. Not at all like a frail boy from the country. But now he was again helpless and angry, a poor country boy, out of his depth in a strange new city.

He gritted his teeth as the shopkeeper's sneering face plagued his mind and blindly continued on the path his anger forced on him, oblivious to his surroundings. *How dare he say such things! He doesn't know how much we've suffered. How* dare *he insult—*

"LOOK OUT, BOY!"

The terrified shout jarred him out of his stupor and he turned around, face-to-face with a swiftly approaching horse-carriage that showed no signs of noticing him, much less of slowing down. It was too late. He had no time to get out of the horses' path. Elijah gave a terrified scream and shut his eyes, not wanting to see his own blood splattered on the cobblestones.

Suddenly, a heavy mass slammed into him, knocking him off his feet and pinning him onto the pavement, his teeth rattling in his head from the impact.

"Ye gotta be daft, boy! D'ye have a death wish?" the body on top of him roared in a guttural voice. Elijah squirmed under the immense weight, and the man rolled off him. Elijah sat up and blinked. A large crowd had gathered around him, chattering and muttering.

"He's fine, no harm done. Nothin' to see here, folks," the man said. The crowd slowly diminished, muttering about suicidal attention-seekers. Elijah heard hurried footsteps and saw Fabian weaving his way through the crowd and running towards him.

"Come on, boy. Ye can't be sittin' in th' middle o' the street th' whole day," the man said, offering Elijah a beefy hand.

Elijah took it, and saw his saviour for the first time. He was a large man, over six feet tall and nearly thrice the width of Elijah. He wore a frayed tweed coat and patched trousers. His head had a light smattering of grey hair near the ears and the bald centre shone under the afternoon sun. Sweat trickled down his forehead and dripped from his hanging jowls onto his green shirt. The man reached into his coat-pocket and pulled out a handkerchief, mopping his face. He adjusted his red cap so as to cover his balding head and said,

"Well? Who are ye with? Bin travellin' around Ol' Lunnon Town alone, have ye?"

Before Elijah could answer, a voice from behind him icily said,

"He's with me."

The man looked past Elijah. His eyes settled on Fabian and there was a flash of recognition, quickly concealed.

"Why, hello sir. Yer boy here's bin up ter all sorts o' mischief, runnin' in front o' carriages, scarin' us bystanders, that sort. Had ter pull him out from under a carriage mesel'."

"I apologise for his unacceptable behaviour. Thank you for your help," Fabian replied, walking towards the man and extending his hand out for a handshake. The man responded by quickly thrusting his hand out too. They shook hands, and Elijah saw him slip a piece of paper into Fabian's palm. Fabian pocketed it with a nod and beckoned Elijah to follow him.

The duo weaved their way through pedestrians and ducked into the closest alley, just by the side of Inglot's Emporium. Elijah peeked through the window and saw the shopkeeper snoring contentedly inside.

Fabian walked into the shadows, Elijah following closely behind. He brought out the note, which was covered in an untidy scribble saying,

"The demon hides in the day
His dirty tricks at night he plays,
You'll find him in the raven's nest
Eight o' clock, wish him my best."

Elijah reread the poem several times, not making any sense of it. However, Fabian's eyes lit up in glee the minute he read the verse.

"Thanks, Ed," he chortled..

Elijah looked on, puzzled.

"What does this mean?"

Fabian turned towards him, as if just noticing his presence.

"That, my friend, is a goldmine of information. Our friend is waiting for us, and we shall pay him a visit."

*

At precisely six o' clock, Fabian and Elijah stood at the opening of the circus's tent. The air was filled with the excited chatter of the other spectators waiting to see the spectacular show. Some irritable children who were tired of waiting whined and tugged at their parents' clothes, demanding candied apples. The heavenly scent of caramel and butter wafted into the air, tugging at Elijah's insides. Fabian noticed his longing look, and bought him one.

"Here, you might as well make the most of it while you can," he said, smiling grimly, and handed Elijah the sweet.

Elijah held the candied apple that he sucked on delightedly, having never tasted such fine confectionery. Fabian, however, stood watching the red-and-white striped tent eagerly. He had been oddly excited after receiving the note earlier that afternoon.

"Pardon my asking," Elijah started, ignoring Fabian's grimace at the prospect of another question, "but what exactly are we here for? What do you want from Raven?"

Fabian pinched the bridge of his nose, pretending not to hear his charge's query.

"Does he have something valuable? Money? Jewels, perhaps?"

At this, Fabian looked up.

"All that glitters is not gold, Elijah. Raven has something much more valuable than metal and stone."

Elijah's eyes grew wide with anticipation.

"He has information," Fabian said. Elijah looked disappointed. Suppressing his indignation at Elijah's lacklustre reaction, he explained, "Raven has information we can't get any other way, important information."

Suddenly, the crowd began to part. A lanky man in a paperboy hat and workman's gloves strode through the partition in the crowd and made his way towards the tent. He reached out and tugged at the rope securing the flap and it fell away, revealing a sliver of the space inside.

The crowd suddenly surged forward, people tripping over each other in their haste to get the best seats. Elijah and Fabian were pummelled from all sides, causing him to drop his apple. Fabian grabbed Elijah's hand and pulled him through the sea of people. After several pushes, shoves and toes being stepped on, they entered the tent.

The tent had looked gigantic from outside, but from inside, it was almost unrealistically massive. The inside of the tent was painted an ink black to match the colour of the night sky and dusted with entire constellations that seemed to swirl as Fabian and Elijah walked towards the seating area. In the centre of the tent lay a large circle of gravel, fenced by thin green railings that towered over Elijah.

"It's to keep the monsters in," Fabian whispered, and Elijah couldn't tell if he was serious. Long rows of seats fanned out from the ring, staircases running directly through them. Several swings and ropes hung from the ceiling of the tent, swinging lightly in the partial breeze. Fabian climbed up a few stairs and chose seats in the third row from the ring. From their seats, they could see *everything*.

A few minutes later, once all the spectators had settled down, a small man with a rotund belly strode into the centre of the ring. He wore an emerald-green cape, and a hat to match. He held up a megaphone decorated with pictures of fireworks.

He cleared his throat loudly and said,

"Ladies and gentlemen, girls and boys. Welcome to Fantazmo's Fantastic Circus!" For such a short man, he had a surprisingly robust voice. "Tonight will be an experience like you have never had before. Prepare to be amazed!"

The man walked away to loud applause and cheers which grew hushed as the acts began. They saw a variety of entrancing performances: sea lions balancing balls on their noses, majestic tigers jumping through rings of fire, trapeze artists swinging through the air like graceful birds and Elijah's favourite – the silly clowns that roamed about making fools of themselves. Fabian seemed vaguely distracted throughout the acts, his eyes flitting expectantly around the audience, but Elijah didn't let his companion's sudden sombre demeanour dilute his enjoyment. He had never seen such magnificent and talented artists, and he planned to enjoy his only chance at doing so.

The last act was announced as being performed by Fantazmo himself. Elijah wondered what he would be performing. Perhaps he'd showcase a few card tricks or something. Onhearing the announcement, Fabian sat up straighter. He scrutinised the ring, waiting for the man to appear, as did all the other members of the audience. Elijah leaned forward in his seat to get a better look, but he continued looking at an empty ring. After a few moments, the crowd grew impatient, muttering and whispering irritably. Just when it seemed as if the crowd was ready to vacate their seats, a slow, easy laugh filled the tent. The sound originated from one of the trapeze's swings. All eyes turned towards it, expecting to see someone standing on it. But there was nobody in sight.

"I'm over here," the voice mocked, a light amusement hinted in its words. Fabian swivelled around in his seat, scouring the tent to no avail.

"Why, hello there!" a man said, a few rows behind

With a cry of disbelief, Elijah whirled around. A man in a suit of deep black with white gloves and a mahogany cane topped with a brass dragon sat beside a little girl. Elijah blanched. He could have sworn the man wasn't there before. The man grinned and, with an elaborate gesture with his hands, he disappeared. The spectators all gasped. They squealed with delight and clamoured to see the man, who had suddenly reappeared in the ring. The man swung his cane in a wide arc and did a little jig, disappearing and reappearing all over the ring. The people gasped in awe and wonder, whooping with joy. Fabian watched the man's every movement like a hawk, his eyes rapidly flitting from one corner to another.

After several minutes of this, the man reappeared in the ring, bowed grandly to the orchestral sound of applause and whistles, and disappeared in mid-bow.

Elijah sat in stunned silence. He knew what he had seen wasn't a simple magic trick. It was definitely not an illusion. He may not have known much, but he certainly knew enough to derive this: that man, the owner of the circus, was an Invisitus.

CHAPTER 7

"I'VE NEVER SEEN anything like that!"

"There's no other explanation; it has to be magic!"

"I can't believe my own eyes. It's a miracle!"

The crowd's awed exclamations engulfed the pair of Invisitae, assaulting their ears. Fabian clenched his fists in an anger that was all too visible, but the entranced bystanders paid no attention. Elijah was puzzled. He did not know why his companion was so angry, and once again thought about his reluctance to tell Elijah about his past.

Fabian strode out of the gate purposefully and Elijah hurried behind him, dashing madly between the other spectators. He didn't want to get lost in an unknown locality. *Especially* not one that was filled with wild animals, captive or not. Fabian slowed his pace and waited for Elijah to catch up.

"What now?" Elijah panted, finally coming to a stop.

"You can't have tired already! We'll have to work at your stamina if you want to survive your training."

Elijah grunted in annoyance and repeated his question. Fabian checked his pocket watch. It was intricately carved and had a strange symbol carved on the lid, a snake swallowing its own tail. Fabian sensed a question and answered with a sigh.

"It's an alchemic symbol, the *ouroboros*. It stands for never-ending possibilities, infinite pathways. Quite fitting, don't you agree?" The pocket-watch clicked open, and Fabian stole a glance at the time.

"Ten to eight. We should hurry."

Fabian dragged Elijah into a sparse clump of trees lining the far end of the fenced-off clearing. They ducked in and out of shadows, keeping close to the fence around the circus tent and its grounds. The area was illuminated by four gaslights that hung from lamp posts and as they moved, monstrous and disfigured silhouettes of the animals concealed in the cages sprang up on the tarps that concealed them.

Elijah ran behind Fabian, eager to meet the circus owner. Fabian stopped abruptly, and took hold of Elijah's hands.

"Hold on tight," he said, before twisting on his heel and teleporting the two away.

Elijah found himself sprawled on the ground once again, and stood up with a huff. He found himself in a copse of trees not unlike the one they had just teleported from, except this time he could see a tall metal fence framing the clearing beyond the thicket. Elijah could vaguely make out large shapes beyond the bars of the fence, but the darkness obscured them from his vision. Once his eyes adjusted to the diffused light, Elijah realised that they had teleported a good way behind the circus and its animal cages; the circus's striped tent still stood proud in the distance.

"Why keep the caravans so far away from the tent?" Elijah voiced his query, puzzled.

Fabian smirked as he surveyed the layout, his eyes settling on the cluster of caravans farther to his right.

"Anonymity and concealment, of course," he said. "After all, what is distance to a man who can cross oceans in a single stride? This place is away from the prying eyes of outsiders. And the rest of his troupe has to camp where he tells them to."

As they made their way towards the camp, Elijah decided to voice the questions that had been plaguing his mind.

"Fabian, back there, in the circus . . ."

"Yes?"

"You seemed so angry when the people named his abilities the work of magic. But why? They don't know any better."

The weight of the question lingered in the air, pressing down on their silence. Elijah waited expectantly for an answer, but none came. Fabian continued on his path as if the question had never been asked, as if Elijah had never even spoken.

They walked on. The fence ended.

"We're here," Fabian said, coming to a stop in front of an intricately carved gate that towered over them eerily. Beyond the gate, in the distance, loomed the dark bulk of a mansion behind dense trees. The gate was made of a series of metal grilles joined together with whorl-like patterns. Fabian placed a hand on one of the metal grilles. The gate was covered in a thin film of rust which came away on Fabian's fingers.

"Iron," he said, drawing his hand back. "The gate is made of iron." Fabian bent his head, his lips curving upwards into the hint of a smile. He turned to Elijah, green eyes gleaming eerily. "You'll want to stand back and watch, this time. I'll show you something this circus never can."

Elijah did as directed, walking backwards without drawing his attention away from Fabian. The man placed his palms upon two bars of the gate. He gripped the metal and tensed his shoulders. Fabian maintained the pose for several seconds, and just when Elijah thought he would burst from anticipation, the most extraordinary thing happened.

The metal of the gate began to ripple, the waves radiating outwards from the bars Fabian had gripped. The solid metal of the gate had been reduced to fluid in Fabian's hands, though – amazingly – it managed to stand upright. Fabian gently bent the bars of the gate outwards, and they responded with a seamless grace till they had made a gap wide enough for a man to pass through. Elijah once again found himself speechless.

Satisfied, Fabian let go of the bars, which instantly resumed their solidity. He turned to face Elijah, cheeks flushed. He took one look at Elijah's gaping face and grinned.

"I'm starting to think that's the only expression you're capable of."

His words jarred Elijah out of his trance, and the boy returned his grin with equal vigour.

"How did you do that? Can all Invisitae do that?"

Fabian smiled.

"All Invisitae have an affinity, a special ability. Mine is controlling metals. All except steel, as I'm sure you remember."

Elijah involuntarily thought of Fabian shackled to the chair with a chain of steel, and how afraid he had looked in that moment. *No wonder*, Elijah thought. The memory seemed so far away, not at all as if it had happened just two days ago.

Fabian looked again at his pocket watch, and his eyes nearly bulged out of his head.

"We have to hurry! There's no time left!"

He grabbed Elijah's hand and ran through the hole in the gate, pulling Elijah behind him. They continued further and found themselves in a deserted area amidst several brightly coloured caravans, their colours just discernable in the light of a few flaming torches clamped to poles stuck in the ground. The meagre light cast a ghostly sheen over the caravans and Elijah peered around, fascinated.

The compound was a ghost town, and tendrils of fear coursed down Elijah's back as they made their way through it. Fabian looked at all the caravans that gleamed in sickly colours under the gaslights, muttering, "Where are you, Raven?" under his breath. His eyes flitted from one caravan to the next, finally landing on the smallest, most inconspicuous one of all. It was one of those things that someone could pass by without even noticing it. It was painted a shade of indigo which had been worn down to the dull greyish blue of frostbite. The curtains were drawn, and there were no telltale signs of life behind the drapes. The only remotely new adornment on the drab caravan was a lock that gleamed in the pale light.

"There it is," Fabian said triumphantly, breaking the deafening silence. Elijah looked in the direction of Fabian's gaze and registered the presence of the dilapidated caravan for the first time.

He made his way to the caravan, kicking up plumes of dust in his haste. Once he stood facing the entrance of the vehicle, he stretched out his right arm, fingers splayed. He then made a crushing motion with his palm, bending the fingers into fists, and Elijah watched with fascination as the lock followed his motions and crumpled in on itself. Fabian opened the door and entered the vehicle, motioning for Elijah to follow him.

The inside of the caravan was pitch-black, the drawn curtains blocking out all light from the gaslights hanging outside. Fabian cursed as he bumped into a hard piece of furniture and rooted around in his coat pocket for something. He grunted with satisfaction and pulled out the cursed dagger that bathed the caravan with pulsating white light. Elijah automatically shied away from the luminous blade. It had brought him nothing but trouble.

The caravan was arranged in a very pristine manner. A small cot lay in the corner furthest from Elijah, neatly done up in white linens. A large armoire sat regally in the opposite corner. To the right of the wardrobe, there was a desk that was covered in neat stacks of paper held together with string. An inkwell was perched precariously on a tower of books with strange titles like, *A Beginner's Guide to Snooping* by Arthur Freeman and *Celebrating Secrets* by Cynthia Brooks as well as some more familiar books, including *A Tale of Two Cities* by Charles Dickens, which Elijah remembered seeing in the neighbouring village's school.

Elijah registered that despite the lack of space in the caravan, it was not cluttered. In fact, it was almost impossibly neat, with everything put away in its rightful position. Except for one notable exception: the door to the armoire was ajar. Elijah started towards the armoire and opened it wide. The armoire was big enough for a grown man to hide in. Inside were three sets of outfits identical to the one worn by "Fantazmo" during his performance, amongst other articles of clothing. Elijah clambered into the wardrobe, his new shoes thunking heavily on the floor of the armoire with a resounding, hollow thud. *That's odd,* Elijah thought, *it's almost as if there's a hollow under this layer of wood.* Excited, he scrabbled at the wooden flooring and found a clasp. He sprang out of the wardrobe, called out for Fabian and asked him to shine the dagger inside it. Elijah unhooked the clasp and raised the platform of wood. Indeed, it was hollow. Soft gleams of light periodically emanated from the hole in the floor, and Fabian pocketed the dagger. Its light was no longer necessary.

Fabian peered into the crevice.

"It seems to be some sort of room," he muttered and looked at the proudly beaming Elijah and ruffled his newly spruced hair. "Good job, lad. Now stay here while I go and find out just why this room exists."

Elijah's face promptly morphed into a scowl. He was expecting a hearty congratulation, not an abrupt dismissal!

"But I *found* it. I should go too," he whined.

Fabian, who had begun lowering himself into the hole, looked up and said, "I swore on my life that I would do all in my power to keep you safe. I don't know about you, but I greatly value my life and I'm not ready to give it up for some snotty brat with a death wish. Now *stay here.*"

Elijah grumbled a retort and sat back, crossing his arms in anger. Fabian rolled his eyes at the display of childish behaviour and dropped down through the trapdoor. At once, Elijah was on his feet. He waited to hear Fabian's footsteps fade away and scrambled back into the wardrobe. He swung his legs into the tunnel below and, giving the inside of the caravan one last glance, jumped through.

*

Elijah landed in a tangle of arms and legs on a soft, dirt floor. He brushed the flecks of mud off him and stood up. He looked up through the trapdoor in the ceiling. It wasn't too high up, but Elijah was uncertain on how he'd get out of the chamber, but he'd cross that bridge when he came to it.

Elijah looked around him. He was standing in a corridor made of damp earth that was lined with velvety green moss. The corridor was very short and not very wide either, but a burning torch in the bracket on the wall lit up the space nicely, allowing Elijah to walk through the tunnel without fear of tripping. The end of the corridor opened out into a narrower tunnel, which ended in a sturdy door made of rowan wood with a missing handle and no keyhole. Elijah espied a twisted shard of metal on the floor near the door and made out that it was the handle. Fabian was most certainly on the other side of the door.

Elijah had seen Fabian when he was murderously angry, and it wasn't a comforting memory. He definitely didn't want to invoke his wrath again. Bearing this in mind, Elijah decided against barging into the room. Instead he placed his ear against the thick wood, catching muffled snippets of a conversation.

"It's quite a set up you have here, Raven." Elijah identified the speaker to be Fabian. "Courtesy of one of your 'friends'?"

Someone else chuckled. The other Invisitus – Raven.

"I simply realised that the best way to hide was in plain sight. No one believes us to be so foolish."

Raven went on,

"I can't believe you're still doing Sapiens's dirty work for him, Fabian. I expected you'd be slightly more enterprising, to say the least."

"Sorry to disappoint," Fabian replied snidely. "Did you get the information I asked for?"

"Yes, I did. And I do believe it will interest you *far more* than you thought it would."

"What do you mean?"

The man's air of pride was tangible. "Now, now, Fabian. Do you have the money I asked for?"

There was the sound of someone rooting around in a pocket, followed by the clinking of coins.

"Forty gold coins. They're all there."

Something flew through the air and landed with a thud. Elijah heard the sound of a drawstring being opened and the jangle of coins as Raven greedily counted them.

"Yes, they do seem to be there. But, alas! What a shame you didn't care to honour the terms of my exchange." Elijah could feel the man's sneer through the thick wood.

"What do you mean? I gave you your money!"

"But you didn't come alone. Someone has followed you. I'll just be taking this money as . . . compensation."

"*That's a lie.* There is no one with me."

"Oh really?"

Elijah felt a change in the atmosphere. He tasted a metallic tang in the air, like that before a storm. Instinctively, he drew back from the door and backed into the corridor. Just in time. Blinding white light blazed through the crevices of the door, and suddenly, it was blown off its hinges. Elijah covered his head as splinters assaulted him like shrapnel. Coloured spots danced before Elijah's eyes and his head throbbed, as if he had been staring unguarded at the sun. Once his vision cleared, he saw the charred remains of what had been a door, and would hardly even pass for firewood now. The force of the explosion had embedded splinters of wood in the floor and walls of the corridor. They'd all missed him, miraculously. Elijah watched on in fascinated horror as one lone surviving slice of wood sizzled and smoked on the dirt floor.

"*Come out, boy! Come out, come out wherever you are!*" a singsong voice dripping with malice floated through the doorway towards Elijah, beckoning him forward. Elijah resisted the pull of the words and retreated further into the corridor.

"Believe me, boy. I'll drag you in here by your ears and beat you bloody if you don't show yourself. *Now.*" The voice was a snarl, and Elijah felt the ice-cold fingers of fear grip his heart. His legs carried him towards the sound of the voice of their

own accord and he was powerless to stop them. Fear drew
him in through the doorway, face to face with Fabian and the
circus master, Fantazmo – or Raven, as Fabian called him.
Raven sneered coldly and the look of stark disbelief plastered
on Fabian's face made Elijah look away. He had let the man
down. Fabian had taught him who he was, had clothed and
fed him, but he had thrown it all back in his face all because
of hubris. Elijah's cheeks were aflame, and he felt himself turn
red from the tip of his toes to the roots of his brown hair.

Raven laughed silkily.

"Well, what have we here? The human beetroot, am I
right?" Elijah turned a deeper shade of crimson. "Your name
is Red, isn't it?"

"It's Elijah."

"As I was saying, *Red*, do you know what I do to
intruders?" Raven abandoned his post beside Fabian and
circled the boy. "Ravens aren't very hospitable birds, you
know. We don't take kindly to *unwanted guests*." His voice
was smooth butter, but it had a dark undertone to it.

"Leave him alone, Raven. He's just a boy." Fabian spoke
for the first time since Elijah's appearance.

"Oh, is that so? *Just a boy*? Well then, we can't have him
tattling about our little secret, can we? No, I didn't think so."
Raven was enjoying his power immensely. He slid one long,
gloved finger under Elijah's chin, and jerked his head upwards.
The man was quite terrifying up close, to say the least. He had
sallow skin that was pulled taut across his cheekbones. The
man had shiny black hair that was slicked back fashionably

and cruel eyes that were darker than the sky in hell itself. They too bore the silver designs that set an Invisitus apart from human beings, but the silver patterns looked like holes in his irises, standing out shockingly against the cold black. His pencil-thin moustache quivered as he scrutinised Elijah's face. In that moment, he really did look like a raven.

After moments of scrutiny, he let go of Elijah's face and turned to face Fabian.

"Well, well. Someone's not being entirely honest, are they?" he addressed the other man. "He isn't just a *boy*."

"You will keep him out of this or I'll rip that sneer off your face. Now *tell me what you know!*"

Malice glinted in Raven's eyes, but he maintained his easy smile.

"You know I used to like you, Fabian. Your skill with all those shiny metals . . . you know that ravens love shiny objects, don't you?" he addressed the question to Elijah, who said nothing. Unperturbed, Raven went on. "You lot are boring me. I won't tell you anything, and sadly, you can't put up much of a fight here, Fabian. I'm afraid our stock on metals is pitifully low." Fabian remained impassive. "As for the boy . . . well, how much of a threat could he be? From the looks of it I'd say he just recently went through the Change. And it takes weeks, no, *months* for an Invisitus to find his affinity. So I'm not worried."

Raven walked in a circle around Elijah, his boots thudding against the earth with every step. "Why, I bet I could electrocute him in my sleep."

Elijah looked up at Fabian. His face was a stoic mask, but he knew what it really hid: defeat, hopelessness, fear. Elijah had seen it in his mother's face every day since before he could remember. He balled his hands into fists and rasped,

"You're wrong."

Raven stopped gloating. "Pardon?"

Elijah looked up, eyes blazing. "You heard me.You're *wrong* to not be worried about me."

A flash of emotion flickered in Raven's eyes. Amusement? But it was quickly replaced by the nonchalant expression he wore so well.

"Quit your babbling, boy. You know nothing. You're just a *child.*"

Elijah seethed. Raven stepped towards Elijah, his lithe body taut with predatory grace. He closed his eyes and reopened them seconds later. Elijah was taken aback. His eyes were like chips of steel, completely silver. Despite himself, Elijah couldn't help his throat constricting with terror. Raven met his eyes, but Fabian placed his body between the two.

Fabian whispered urgently,

"Back away slowly, and then run. Do you understand?"

"He's right, boy. You should run." He paused, his skin stretching across his bones as he bared his teeth. "But I'm afraid I can't let that happen. Curiosity is a sin, didn't you know? It deserves punishment."

Raven removed his gloves and clasped his palms together, as if he was praying. Fabian nudged Elijah with his shoulder, pushing him closer to the gaping hole in the wall where the door once stood. But Elijah was done running. He gave into the fear and rage that coursed through his veins and tried to invoke the trance he'd been trapped in at Inglot's Emporium. He thought of the life he'd left behind, the sacrifices he'd made. He thought of his mother whom he'd never seen cry, and of how much his desertion of her must have hurt her. But most of all, he thought about the life he'd given up. He'd never asked to be an Invisitus. He'd had no choice in the matter. An overpowering wave of sorrow and rage engulfed him. Maybe he wanted to stay human, or maybe he *would have* liked to lead the life of an Invisitus.

All he'd wanted was a choice.

Suddenly, his vision turned silver. His heart leapt and he felt flushed, adrenaline coursing through his veins, his senses heightened. He felt the wind pick up around him, and he willed it to carry him up towards the ceiling. He could see Fabian watching, thunderstruck, and saw Raven aiming his outstretched palms in Elijah's direction. Elijah felt the shift in the air and tasted the metallic tang on his tongue. He saw a bright flash of light building between Raven's palms, and felt the air around him get charged with a palpable verve. His blood quickened in response to the latent energy surrounding him, and Elijah felt it pulse with electrifying energy.

The dry wind whipped Elijah's newly groomed hair around his face, and snapped at Raven's clothes. The crackle of light energy in Raven's hands was getting stronger. Elijah felt electricity crackle down his arms, and spark around his fingers. The wind howled and whipped Raven's slick hair out of shape, but the man paid no attention, concentrating on the growing orb of light between his palms. Elijah's arms numbed with power, and red spots danced in the corners of his eyes. Just a few more seconds . . .

*

Fabian watched in profound horror at the scene unfolding around him. He shouted a warning to Elijah, but the keening of the wind blew his words out of earshot scarcely before they'd left his lips. The gale was fantastically strong, and nearly swept Fabian off his feet. The wind was in a frenzy around Elijah, obscuring the boy from view completely. Fabian shielded his eyes with his palms, trying to block out the growing flashes of light building in Raven's palms.

Suddenly, blinding tendrils of light shot out of Raven's hands and coursed towards Elijah. Fabian's heart leapt into his throat. The light hit the tornado of wind around Elijah, and ricocheted back towards the figure that was Raven. Raven swerved at the last minute, the blazing lightning scorching the ends of his dishevelled hair and buried itself in the wall behind him, splintering the stone.

Raven laughed manically, but the confident gleam in his eyes had muted into a smattering of fear. He took his stance once more, and called down another bolt of lightning. The smell of ozone tickled Fabian's nostrils, and he watched in horror as the finger of light travelled straight at Elijah.

All of a sudden, an arc of blue light shot out from behind the tornado, and met the prong of lightning emanating from Raven's hands with the deafening crash of shattering glass. Fabian fell and scrabbled at the grooves in the stone floor, hastily crawling away from the growing column of light which crackled with fissures of lightning.

The energy emanating from the column of coalescent blue and white light was so potent that it whistled and sang, drowning out even the howling of the wind. Elijah's brows knit together as he concentrated on making the blue light envelop and extinguish Raven's own lightning.

Raven's features contorted into a mask of fear and concentration, and sweat poured off his face in rivulets as he fought to keep the growing beam of blue light away from him. His arms faltered under the strain, and his knees buckled, but the boy stood resolute. He looked at Elijah with abject terror.

"What are you?" he whispered.

As an answer, Elijah thrust his arms forward and the blue lightning surged towards Raven, completely obliterating Raven's own beam of energy. With a cry, Raven threw up his hands in a feeble attempt to protect himself from the oncoming lightning, and sank to the ground.

The blue light stopped inches away from his closed eyelids, crackling menacingly and flickering across his skin, making the ghostly pallor appear corpselike in its blue aura.

Elijah snapped his fingers, and the lightning reeled away from its victim, springing back to Elijah's fingertips obediently, before disintegrating in a shower of blue sparks. Raven babbled incoherently as a wet spot grew on the front of his trousers.

Fabian jarred himself out of his stupor and ran towards Raven, who lay moaning on the ground.

"Tell me. *What did you find out?*" Fabian snarled.

"They have Invisitae spies . . . Stronghold in Wales . . . Dagger . . . *Occidierum!*" Raven mumbled fragments of sentences as he clutched his steaming shoulder. Fabian wasn't reassured by the newly acquired information, but it was information all the same. He reached into his coat pocket and brought out the bloodlace. Its delicate petals were slightly crushed, but it would still do. He threw it at Raven and turned to face Elijah.

The boy's silvered eyes glinted with menace, residual sparks from the lightning dancing in them. Fabian stepped warily towards the suspended figure and called the boy's name.

A flash of recognition crossed his features, and the silver of his eyes began receding back into the patterns on his iris. The boy spiralled downwards, and landed heavily on his feet.

His gaze unfocused, he said,

"Did I just—?"

Fabian smiled with relief that his charge was alright.

"Yes, you did."

Elijah tried to smile, but it resembled a grimace instead.
"I—I—I—"

He pitched forward, and Fabian ran to catch him before he hit the ground.

CHAPTER 8

ELIJAH STOOD AT the foot of a cliff overlooking the sea. The choppy grey waters churned and boiled like a witch's brew, waves crashing against the jagged face of the crag and sending sea spray shooting upwards to meet the sky, which retaliated with equal intensity by sending rain down in blinding sheets. The torrents of rain stung his skin and chilled him to the bone. Wind lashed at him, whipping his hair across his face. Forks of lightning sprang out of the clouds like arrows crackling with electric fire and the rumble of thunder made the rocks beneath his feet quiver.

He turned and looked behind him, agape at the large metallic tower that loomed over him threateningly at the edge the cliff above him. A soggy dirt path ran up the cliff, leading all the way till the lip of the cliff that rose over the sea. Elijah heard muffled laughter over the howling wind. *It came from the cliff-top*, Elijah thought, toiling up the path. The wind put up a valiant fight and deterred him from reaching the origin of the laughter, but in the end he made it to the top. But it soon made him wish he hadn't.

A girl no older than Elijah stood at the very edge of the cliff, her face frozen in a mask of fear. He looked at her in confusion, doing a double-take when he realised that there was a shadowy figure standing behind her and holding a dagger to her throat. He saw the girl gulp as the knife drew scarlet blood from her throat, the figure behind her laughing with crazed glee. The man took the girl a step closer to the uneven edge, her foot kicking fragments of rock into the ocean.

Elijah stood frozen in place, the infernal shrieks of wind voicing his own despair. Elijah could do nothing but stare at the girl as she was dragged nearer and nearer to the edge of the cliff. She had wild auburn curls that rested on her shoulders, the wind and rain plastering the ringlets to her temples. Piercing violet eyes gazed out of her pale impish face. Elijah's shoulder tensed as he realised what the man was attempting to do, and he stumbled towards the helpless girl.

But a moment too late, for the man nimbly turned around and flung the girl away from him, laughing as she fell towards the sea like a rock, the waves rising up to pull her into her watery grave . . .

"NO!"

Elijah woke up screaming, drenched in sweat. His heart thumped rapidly against his ribs, his throat constricting painfully. Never had he had such a vivid dream. A nightmare, rather. He felt himself lying on a hard, lumpy mattress that had rendered him stiff and irritable. He had been propped up on pillows that were equally uncomfortable and covered in a thin blanket that served as asheet. He wore a scratchy tunic several sizes too large, and a pair of drawstring pants. He had no idea where he was or how he had gotten here, but just the feel of a bed underneath him calmed him down. His heart's beating settled into a slow rhythm and he raised a hand to wipe the sweat from his brow, but found that he could not. Upon closer inspection, he saw his wrists and ankles shackled in steel manacles, bound to a four-poster bed. Elijah struggled against his bindings and, after several draining attempts, he fell back against the pillows, breathing hard. He looked around him helplessly.

Elijah had been confined in a room with a relatively low ceiling from which hung a single lamp that threw a sickly light around the room. The walls had been painted a drab beige, the paint cracked and peeling in places. A closed door stood directly opposite the bed. The room was sparsely furnished. A once-elegant table that had been eaten away by termites stood near his bed, an unlit tallow candle placed upon it. A plain cupboard also stood alone in the corner furthest from the door to the room, but that was it.

His heart leapt in his chest. Elijah was shackled to a bed in an unknown place. He recalled no memory of getting there, let alone knew where *there* was. Panicked, he began shouting for help, but his calls went unanswered. He felt his eyes swim with tears, his vision going blurry. He could hold them back no longer. Elijah felt panic and fatigue overcome him, and he succumbed to tears that traced paths of ice down his cheeks. For the first time in his life, Elijah felt truly and utterly alone.

*

Elijah swam in and out of consciousness, his head whirling with questions. *How did I get here? What is this place? Where's Fabian?* He desperately wanted to slip back into the arms of sleep, but the pestering questions kept it at bay.

"Psst!"

Elijah swivelled his head, scouring the room for the origin of the whisper.

"Down here! Under the bed!" called out a disembodied voice.

Elijah craned his neck to peer over the sides of the bed, but his bonds held fast. He groaned loudly in frustration.

"Who are you?" He could almost see the hidden person cringing.

"Not so loud!" the voice hissed, "they'll hear you."

"*Who* will hear me?" he inquired.

There was an audible hiss of frustration.

"*Them.* Quick! Pretend you're asleep. And whatever you do," the voice took on a warning tone, "*don't tell them anything.*"

The voice grew hushed, and Elijah heard the sound of nearing footsteps. Quickly, he feigned unconsciousness and slumped back onto the pillows. The footsteps paused at the door.

". . . How could he use his power so soon, Lucian?" Elijah heard an agitated man say.

"Patience, Surazal. All will be answered in due time." A much calmer baritone replied. His words, though not uttered loudly, seemed to fill the room and filled Elijah with a rejuvenating sense of calm.

"But—"

"That's enough. We mustn't disturb the boy," Lucian, the man with the baritone voice, said with an air of finality. "He was completely drained of energy when Fabian brought him to us. He must have performed a formidable feat indeed."

The men entered the chamber and Elijah began breathing slowly and deeply, a precise imitation of a sleeping figure, but cracked open his eyes a fraction. They were both of considerable height, but the one named Surazal towered over the shorter, older man. The men wore identical silver robes with full-length sleeves and cuffs inscribed with spidery glyphs that were unreadable to Elijah. The fabric rippled as they made their way towards the bed, like metallic water.

"But it's been three days! We have to investigate further. If Sapiens's vision is correct, he could be the death of us all!"

Through half-lidded eyes, Elijah saw the older man's greying brows furrow.

"I have done what I can to speed up his recovery. But since this is not an ailment, I'm afraid there is little I can do."

Surazal scowled. Elijah hastily shut his eyes as Surazal bent down and scrutinised Elijah's face. He hoped the frantic thumping of his heart was not audible.

Elijah heard a rustle of fabric as Surazal straightened. He dared not open his eyes again.

"Very well. We shall allow him till evening to recuperate. We have very many questions, and not nearly enough time to get answers."

He made his way to the door.

"Surazal . . ." the older man called out. "Is it true that the Occidierum have other Invisitae amongst our ranks? Fabian said he was attacked by one of them."

Surazal ceased walking.

"Yes," he said. He exited the room.

Lucian patted Elijah's shoulder comfortingly, but his face betrayed his confusion.

"But how?" he said and followed his companion out of the room, leaving his question unanswered.

*

Elijah looked around his once again seemingly deserted room and whispered loudly,

"You can come out now."

"I *know*," the voice barked back irritably. There was the sound of a body scrambling out from under the bed accompanied by muffled grunts of frustration. Elijah anxiously awaited the appearance of his visitor. The voice sounded feminine and faintly familiar to Elijah's ears, though he didn't know from where.

A slim figure crawled out from under the bed. Elijah craned his neck and caught a glimpse of startlingly bright red hair tumbling wildly down her shoulders, contrasting shockingly against her bottle-green tunic. She brushed off dust from her black drawstring trousers, back turned towards Elijah. A thought popped into Elijah's head. *Could she be . . . No, that's impossible.*

But, indeed, she was.

The girl turned around, her face split into a wide grin exposing pearly white teeth. Elijah was taken aback; her violet eyes burned with an intensity that made him want to look away, but he held her gaze. They stared at each other warily for several seconds, a dangerous dance of pointed looks. Elijah looked away.

"Thanks for that," the girl said, still grinning. "They'd kill me if they found out I was here! But I had to see for myself."

Elijah took in her ecstatic face, puzzled.

"See what?"

"If you were really the Stormbringer. Why else?"

"The Stormbringer?" Elijah was growing more confused by the second. He felt very silly. He had grown well acquainted with the feeling in the past few days.

The girl looked at him incredulously.

"You really don't know a thing, do you?"

Elijah was about to reply when he was cut off by an unknown voice.

"As well as he should."

The girl's face turned a violent shade of red, not unlike her hair, and looked sheepishly at a figure standing behind Elijah. The boy whipped his head round to look at the man, and stared. The man was clothed in garments similar to Elijah's previous visitors, but the spidery runes were not limited to his garment. They stained the skin on his exposed arms and neck, whorls of raised silvery-pink welts as if someone had gouged them in with a knife. He had long white hair that hung below his shoulders in a snaking plait. His gaunt face was lined with creases and wrinkles, indicating his obvious age. However, his flint-grey eyes were sharp and focused. He gave a pointed look to the cowering girl who blushed a deeper red, then turned his gaze to Elijah. Instantly, his face softened, his high cheekbones melting into the wrinkles on his face. He broke into a warm smile, skin crinkling under his eyes. Elijah could tell this man smiled a lot.

"I see you've met Adara," the man said in a rich baritone, indicating the girl.

"I suppose so." Elijah said. He jangled the shackles holding him in place. His hands were numb from being trapped for so long.

The elderly man noticed his discomfort.

"Ah, I almost forgot about those!" He placed his palms on the metal shackles holding Elijah captive, talking all the while. "So very sorry for going to such extreme measures. The Manor can be quite dangerous for a person who has no idea how to navigate it. We wouldn't want you to go running off into a chamber without floors now, would we?" he said, smiling. Elijah gazed at his hands, dumbstruck, as the shackles holding him fell off with a resonant click.

"You can manipulate metals too?" Elijah inquired.

The man laughed heartily.

"No, my boy. I do not share the same affinity with Fabian. I can simply unlock anything. Doors, shackles, minds. *Anything.*" He smiled at Elijah's growing sense of awe.

"Sapiens! You need to hurry to the entrance immediately!" a voice rang out, followed by footsteps. A short man wearing plaid trousers and a frayed jacket ran into the room, his distress plain for all to see.

Sapiens left the children and strode towards the man, his silver robes flowing about his feet.

"Calm down, Atticus, and speak clearly. What seems to be the matter?"

The man took a few gulps of air before answering.

"Zachariah is back. *They* sent him back."

Sapiens paled, his scars livid against his pale skin.

"Very well. I shall make haste." He looked over his shoulder at the children who were watching the encounter with rapt attention.

"Adara, take Elijah to the Sanctuary. Fabian will be waiting for him." She began protesting, but he silenced her with a look. "Avoid the west wing." Sapiens turned to Elijah. "My boy," he hesitated, then looked away. "Stay safe."

And with that, the men swept out of the room, leaving it empty once again.

CHAPTER 9

ELIJAH WAS QUICKLY beginning to realise that there was no worse torture than being trapped in an unknown place with an infuriated girl. They navigated through endless cream-coloured corridors that looked identical to one another and Elijah worried they'd been walking fruitlessly in circles. Adara stalked ahead of him, arms crossed, fuming. Once in a while Elijah caught her muttering bitter words under her breath. Fragments of angry statements assaulted his ears repeatedly, until he finally confronted her.

"Adara?"

"WHAT?"

The girl whipped around to face Elijah, glaring murderously at him. Elijah took a nervous step back.

"Why are you so angry at Sapiens?"

Adara stood up straight.

"You will address him as Eldest Sapiens. He is the leader of our people. Pay him the respect he deserves." She hesitated, then continued, "He never lets me out of his sight! And at the first sign of danger, he sends me back to seek shelter with the matrons. He never lets me fight, even when that's what I've been trained to do! He treats me like a helpless child."

Elijah certainly wouldn't perceive Adara as helpless, but she was still a child. Nevertheless, he decided this was the wrong time to mention it.

"No, I'm not," Adara said, gritting her teeth. Elijah looked at her, puzzled.

"You aren't what?" he asked.

She looked up to meet his gaze, visibly startled.

"Nothing, nothing at all." She regained her composure and signalled Elijah to follow her deeper into the labyrinth of passages.

They walked on and on.

"Why can't we just teleport to the Sanctuary?"

"Teleporting without an adult Invisitus is strictly forbidden," she recited in a bitter monotone. Then, with a significantly brighter tone she said, "then again, rules *are* made for breaking . . ." she halted abruptly, her features screwing with concentration, as if she were arguing with herself.

Elijah followed Adara silently as she led him towards the place Eldest Sapiens had called the Sanctuary. He looked around him in awe; never had he entered a passageway so endless. His footsteps sounded sharply against the marble floors, echoing off the high, vaulted ceiling. Elijah marvelled at the grandeur of the passage, but was brought out of his reverie when someone cleared their throat. Elijah saw that they had reached a threshold of sorts, a doorway that signified the end of the labyrinth. Beyond, he could see plain teakwood floors worn smooth by the scores of feet that marched across it.

"We're here," Adara droned. "Welcome to the Sanctuary."

Elijah stepped across the threshold and felt the air change its consistency. It was a strange sensation, like walking through honey, and disappeared when Elijah walked further into the room. Adara followed him in, muttering under her breath. If she felt the shift in the air, she didn't indicate it.

"A protective charm," Adara said, almost as if she read the question off his mind. "The Sanctuary is protected against all mortals, and this barrier keeps the humans out. Not that it's going to be of much use, if what Surazal said is true."

"Where's Fabian?" Elijah enquired, looking around the bare room.

"I don't know," Adara said, equally curious. "I can't feel his presence." She quickly realised what she had said and looked away from Elijah's gaze.

"I'm here." A familiar voice called out, stepping out from behind a pillar. "And you, Adara, need to pay a bit more attention in training," he added, smiling.

"You have to be around to make sure I do." She returned his grin broadly.

Elijah watched them carefully. Adara seemed to change around Fabian, not so much like a taut whip and more like a child their age.

"Fabian's one of my closest friends. He's one of my mentors," she explained, addressing Elijah. "You'll be assigned your own mentor soon." He nodded, understanding.

"How are you feeling? That was a pretty impressive fight you put up, there." Fabian's voice held traces of a strange emotion. *Admiration*, Elijah realised with a start.

"I'm better now. But is this normal? Fainting every time you use your affinity?" Elijah asked.

A few seconds passed, and Fabian and Adara exchanged looks, almost as if they were having an unspoken conversation. Fabian sighed and said,

"No. But then again, you haven't undergone any training. So you can't be expected to control any power surges."

Elijah listened to Fabian, but knew something was off. The man was lying through his front teeth. Nonetheless, he decided not to press for answers. Let them think he believed them.

"What on earth do we have here?" a stern feminine voice called out. Elijah turned to face the corridor at the opposite end of the room, and came face to face with a stout woman standing in the doorway. She wore a starched white dress that hid every inch of her plump body. Her greying hair was scraped back into a neat bun, not a hair out of place. Stern lines punctuated her severe face as she took in the scene before her in disapproval, looking over the tops of her round spectacles. Elijah could tell at once that she wasn't one to take lightly.

"Well then, answer me! What are you all doing down here? Adara, you are supposed to be in training with Zeli right now! Don't tell me you decided to skip his session. And Fabian, you let her get away with it? What a fine example you're setting your charge." She turned towards Elijah, who stepped back worriedly. "And who are you?"

Elijah stammered out his name. Suddenly, the lines in the woman's face softened, shaking off her stern image.

"Ah, the newest member of the Brotherhood. So nice to meet you. My name is Alma." Without waiting for a reply, she turned back to scolding Adara. "Well then, what excuse are you going to feed me now? You'd think that reserve would have been exhausted by now."

Adara spoke without hesitation:

"Zachariah is back."

There was a sharp intake of breath as the woman's hand flew to her heart.

"Well then, we'd better get the boy to his own quarters. Come along." She turned and went back through the corridor she had come from, and the others followed her through.

"Who is Zachariah?" Elijah asked Fabian.

Fabian didn't look at Elijah, and waited several seconds before replying.

"A traitor who should have been long dead."

*

The group walked down a long corridor with a slight upwards incline. They followed the main body of the corridor, ignoring the branches. They passed by several women clad in white dresses like Alma, ranging from the mid-twenties to late sixties, carrying baskets of washing and rich-smelling dishes. They smiled warmly at Elijah as they went about their way. Elijah's stomach grumbled. He didn't know how many meals he had skipped. Alma turned around, her eyes widening.

"My, we have quite the monster in our belly, don't we?" Elijah blushed. "Don't you fret, child. We'll fatten you up soon enough." Adara smirked as Elijah's blush deepened.

After a brisk walk down a branch on the left side of the corridor, they emerged into a cavernous room. Like the corridor, it had wooden floors and pale pastel walls. A large wooden bed stood in the centre of the room, flanked by an armoire and a small table. Two chairs faced the bed. *Strange*, Elijah mused, *no windows, just like the rest of the rooms in this place.*

Fabian seemed to divine his question and obliged.

"As you may have noticed, there is a significant lack of windows at the Manor. That is because we are, in fact, underground."

Elijah's eyes widened. But he wasn't too surprised. An underground dwelling was the least exciting part of his life now.

"I wouldn't be so sure," Adara said pointedly, as though on cue, ignoring the startled look Elijah threw her. "I think you'll find that there are several surprises hidden within these halls, not all of them pleasant."

"And please don't go around looking for trouble," Alma added warningly.

Elijah walked over and sat down on the bed and Fabian and Adara sank into the plush chairs opposite him. Alma announced that she'd send up some supper, and went about her way.

"Knowing you, that can't be the last of your questions," Fabian addressed Elijah.

"Well, why is an entire mansion located underground?" Elijah asked.

"What we are inhabiting now is a network of passages and rooms built under the ruins of the Penvellyn mansion. You see, the mansion was destroyed when Sir Robert Penvellyn first attempted to make the Philosopher's Stone. Instead, he manufactured an elixir called tainted water. It failed to make humans immortal, but it did succeed in creating our abilities," Fabian answered.

"So the Invisitae were born of alchemy?"

"Yes, that is correct."

Elijah was about to ask another question when a man ran into Elijah's quarters, gasping for breath. His eyes were dilated with fear as he choked on his words.

"The boy is being summoned. Zachariah demands to see him."

Fabian stood up, indignant.

"And Eldest Sapiens agreed? What is he thinking?"

The man nodded, then looked at Adara, whose face was a mask of concentration. She broke out of her reverie and said, "He must go meet with Zachariah. Eldest won't tell me why, but it seems important."

Fabian reluctantly agreed. He made his way to the doorway, but the messenger stopped him.

"No time," he wheezed. Then, without warning, he took hold of Elijah and Fabian's hands and they vanished into thin air, leaving behind a very disappointed Adara.

CHAPTER 10

ELIJAH HAD THOUGHT he'd be used to the sensation of weightlessness that accompanied teleportation, but he couldn't have been more wrong. It was like flying through a corridor of fragmented images like shards of glass. The sensation lasted for a fraction of a second, and then they were catapulted into a great hall. It had marbled floors and a high ceiling etched with the words *Vias nostras infinitam.* Elijah vowed to find out the meaning of those words soon. He looked around him and saw that he was encircled by several men dressed in silver robes. Elijah recognised the men Lucian and Surazal amongst a sea of unfamiliar faces, and could also identify Eldest, with his tattooed arms.

The man next to Eldest, however, could not have been more out of place. He wore a black dress shirt with smart black trousers. A champagne-coloured cape flowed over his back gracefully, and hovered above the heels of his shiny black boots. His face was all angles. Icy grey eyes stared at Elijah from between sharp eyebrows as the man stroked his goatee thoughtfully.

"That's *him*?" he said, faintly amused. "Well, he's not much, is he?"

"It's a shame you couldn't make it earlier. You wouldn't be quite so surprised," Fabian snarled back.

"Keep that filthy scum away from me, Sapiens. He looks like he might tear a hole through my cape. It's velvet, you know," the man said, raising his nose into the air as though he had caught a whiff of something nasty. Fabian looked like he would do just that but he restrained himself, a muscle jumping in his jaw.

"I hate to interrupt, but he's here now. You had best say what you came here to, and leave," Eldest Sapiens said, walking into the circle to face Zachariah, putting himself between the man and the boy.

"How very blunt. I remember when you used to speak kindly to your apprentice," Zachariah said, reminiscing. "But we have come a long way."

Eldest said nothing, as the circle of men watched with rapt attention. Zachariah strolled at a leisurely pace round Eldest.

"Well, I came for him, of course. Lazarus was very curious to see what I thought about our so-called 'bane'. He needn't have worried. This boy has no chance of facing off against us."

Fabian hissed at the mention of the name, Lazarus, as did several other Elders. Elijah wondered why. The name was unfamiliar to him.

"Lazarus! That filthy name must never be uttered in these halls," a burly elder called out, staring Zachariah down.

Zachariah smirked, and turned to face Elijah once again.

"I think the bane has every right to hear the name of his sworn enemy."

Elijah stepped out from behind Eldest. He didn't like the sound of the word bane.

"Bane? What's that?"

Zachariah's laugh echoed against the domed ceiling of the room.

"*That* is you. The saviour of your people, the destroyer of ours. The Stormbringer."

Elijah's eyes widened.

"I'm no destroyer. I'm just a boy from the country."

The man's eyes widened in mock horror.

"Surely they must have told you!" Registering Elijah's blank look, he smiled evilly. "Of course they didn't. The Brotherhood has a nasty habit of keeping its secrets."

Sapiens raised a hand.

"There's no need for that now, Zachariah. Leave at once."

Zachariah's grin broadened and his eyes grew maniacal.

"Oh, but there is! The most urgent need, in fact. A boy from the country or not, you have a dark heart in you. You may be called a harbinger of justice by some . . ." he looked pointedly at Sapiens, whose tense stature betrayed anxiety,". . . but you will be nothing short of a killer."

Elijah blanched at his words, and the man approached him. Laying a hand on his shoulder, he looked at Elijah. Suddenly, he squinted his cruel eyes, and Elijah gasped at the feeling of an alien consciousness brushing his mind.

"What's this? They've been lying to all of us," he said. "They've been lying all this time." He turned back to Sapiens, who was trying hard to remain expressionless.

Zachariah cocked his head to one side, as if listening to whispers carried by the still air.

"There is someone else. Isn't there?"

Confusion flitted across the faces of all the Elders and heated whispers filled the room. Sapiens stood up taller in an attempt to hide his pallor. Elijah looked from one face to the other, wondering what was going on.

Zachariah took in the dismayed looks on the faces of the Elders and laughed a rich, throaty laugh.

"As Eldest of the Brotherhood, I command you to leave *at once*." Sapiens's eyes began going silver, and Elijah's stomach roiled with fear. He suspected Sapiens was not one to lose his bearings very easily, and that when he did, he would be a force to be reckoned with.

Zachariah clutched at his heart, pretending to look offended.

"Who would've thought you were speaking to your would-be successor as Eldest. Not that I would want to be associated with your kind, mind you."

At Zachariah's words, Fabian teleported away from the circle of elders and appeared a split-second later in front of Zachariah, his teeth bared.

"You forget that you are one of us in kind, if not in spirit," he whispered, his voice laden with malice.

"Not for long, you mangy mutt." Zachariah teleported away from Fabian, taking advantage of the confusion that clouded his features.

"Don't worry, *Eldest*. Your secret is safe with me." Elijah jumped upon hearing the words, as he couldn't see the man they emanated from.

Eldest Sapiens's eyes had glazed over completely, and Elijah felt the thrum of his powerful aura grow as it scoured the room for the invisible Invisitus. Elijah heard a strange whoosh as Sapiens found Zachariah and nullified his shroud of invisibility.

He reappeared at the edge of the circle of Elders, lowering his head in a deep bow meant for Elijah.

"We'll see each other soon enough," he said, and vanished.

Fabian strode to Elijah, followed by Lucian, and put a reassuring arm round his shoulders. Sapiens glanced fleetingly at the boy and turned away. But through his clouded thoughts, Elijah saw the brief emotion of fear flit across his features.

"What did he mean, 'not for long'? Does this mean they have a cure?" Fabian asked, wide-eyed.

An Elder with a shaven head said, "Hush, Fabian. We are not ailing; we have no need for a cure."

The Elder with cat-like eyes interrupted their squabble.

"Ailing or not, Zachariah suggests that the Occidierum can now reverse our condition."

"That's impossible!" another cried.

"Evidently not," another interjected.

Elijah sighed. He was sitting alone in a corner of the room as the Elders of the Brotherhood and Fabian conversed in agitated tones. He caught the terms *fountain* and *Occidierum* but he could make no sense of them. His mind reeled from the recent encounter. He had been nothing but ordinary, and suddenly he was thrown headlong into the whirlwind that was his life at the present. Brother Lucian kept throwing worried glances at him, until finally he excused himself from the discussion and shuffled towards Elijah.

"You seem a little under the weather. Have you a headache?" Lucian asked kindly.

For the first time, Elijah noticed a dull throbbing at his temples. He nodded. Lucian rolled up his sleeves.

"May I?" heasked.

Elijah nodded, and Lucian placed two fingers on Elijah's temples. Suddenly, Elijah felt a rush of warmth spread from the man's fingers, dissolving the throbbing in his head. Instantly, he felt better. Lucian drew back his hand. Elijah realised that his affinity must be healing.

"That must have been a right nasty shock. Zachariah is quite . . . unstable. He can unnerve the bravest of people."

Elijah looked at the kind-eyed man and asked a question that was bothering him immensely.

"He said you were hiding something. What exactly did he mean by that?"

There it was again. Fear flitted across his face so fast, that it was barely noticeable. But Elijah's eyes weren't deceiving him. He did not know whether Lucian would have responded, but before he could, the group disbanded and made their way over. Elijah stood up as they lined up in front of him, a smouldering Fabian falling towards the end of the line.

"Elijah, we are sorry you had to undergo that,"Sapiens said. "It was unfair on my part; yes, you will accomplish great deeds in the future, but you mustn't burden yourself with them today." Elijah smiled weakly.

"Pardon me, Eldest," he squeaked, intimidated, "but what exactly did Zachariah mean when he said that I was the Stormbringer?"

Eldest furrowed his brow.

"I had wished to tell you this myself after you had been trained up slightly, but destiny does work in mysterious ways." He sighed, and Elijah waited patiently.

"For all the good we try and accomplish, we Invisitae have many enemies. Far too many. Hence, years and years before even *my* time, it was prophesised that, when we needed him the most, an Invisitus with the power to bring forth blue light and storm to the earth would grace our Brotherhood, and protect us from annihilation. I heard you put on quite a show for Raven." He winked.

"Your lightning . . . I've never seen anything like it. Blue as the ocean, it was," Fabian said, eyes shining with pride.

Elijah felt the pang of fear, remembering the utter lack of control he'd felt while harnessing the lightning. He'd wielded power so strong, he could scarcely contain it. And to protect an entire race of people . . . He couldn't possibly accomplish what they wanted, what they *needed* him to do.

Eldest sensed his wariness.

"Elijah, my boy. It *is* you," he said. "There have been people before you with immense power, but nothing like that of your calibre." He paused. "With the growing strength of the Occidierum, and the sudden flush of our own kind amongst their ranks, we need the Stormbringer more than ever." Elijah heard the urgency of his words, but Sapiens put it aside and continued.

"Of course, you can't expect to be fighting ready in an instant. Before you can assume the responsibility of the Stormbringer, it is our duty to train you. For a start, you must be assigned a mentor. Being the Stormbringer, you must be assigned with one who is more than capable of protecting you, such as one of us Elders. With due consideration, the Elders have decided that Brother Surazal be named your mentor."

The man who had accompanied Lucian to Elijah's room stepped forward. He smiled at Elijah, but his smile didn't reach his golden eyes that blazed with a fierce light, contrasting vividly with his dark, unruly hair.

Eldest continued,

"Being gifted with the affinity of strength and agility, he is more than suited for this job. From now, your progress in training must be reported to him. Should a transgression be performed on your part, he will decide your punishment as he sees fit."

At this, Surazal's smirk broadened to a smile, and Elijah shuffled nervously on his feet.

"We will be fast friends, Elijah. I can tell," he said. "Come along now, it's almost time for supper. This way you'll get a chance to meet the other boys your age."

*

The line for supper was quite short. It seemed that the Elders and Elijah were the only ones who hadn't already been seated. Elijah stood nervously behind Surazal,scanning the crowd of approximately sixty Invisitae for a familiar face. Finally, he spotted Adara chatting amicably with a group of children around her age, perhaps a few years older.

"Do you understand?" Surazal addressed Elijah, who looked back apologetically. He hadn't heard a word.

A spark of irritation flitted across his mentor's face, so faint that Elijah almost missed it. But Surazal smiled and repeated,

"You take your food and find a seat somewhere I can keep an eye on you. After that, you will follow the other children and receive your training schedule. Half an hour of dilly-dallying and then lights out, you hear?" Surazal stared at Elijah sternly. "And whatever you do, *don't roam the corridors at night*. It isn't safe. Especially not at this time."

Elijah nodded as Surazal turned his back to him and strode to one of the women handing out bowls of food. Elijah mimicked his action and smiled at the lady who handed him a steaming bowl of rice and stew. It looked appetising enough, and smelled divine to Elijah; the last thing he remembered eating was the caramelised apple, and who knows how long ago that had been. He looked over to Adara's table and met her gaze. She beamed at him and waved him over. The boys facing her turned around and looked at Elijah, smiling welcomingly.

Elijah shuffled towards the long table at which they were seated, glad that he had a place to sit. Suddenly, Elijah tripped over something and fell to the ground, his bowl flying out of his hands and shattering as it hit the ground. The room fell silent. A scarlet blush seeped into his cheeks as he picked himself off the ground. He heard sniggers behind him and turned to see a group of older boys laughing into their bowls of stew. One boy, however, smirked steadily at Elijah his cold, grey eyes fixed on Elijah. Elijah looked away, and conversations resumed.

Mortified, Elijah dropped to the ground, making an attempt to clear up the mess he had made on the floor. He tried to hide his scarlet face with his hair, but remembered that his locks had recently been sheared. He reached out for a shard of the broken bowl but withdrew his hand as another hand swiped it up before Elijah could reach it. He looked up, directly into the face of a dark-haired boy with large brown eyes. He smiled slightly and offered a hand, which Elijah took and stood up.

"Stand back," the boy said, and waved his hands towards the mess. Suddenly, the shards of china and morsels of food rose into the air. Elijah watched as the pieces knitted themselves together and the bowl refilled with his supper.

Satisfied, the boy reached out for the bowl and handed it back to Elijah.

"Come along, then," the boy gestured for Elijah to join him at the table where Adara, he and the other children his age sat, and Elijah obeyed. He sat down at an empty space on the bench, opposite Adara.

"That was a nasty fall. Are you alright?" Adara said, commiseratingly. Elijah nodded and sat down. The boy sitting next to him interjected,

"We saw what actually happened. It was Sebastian. He tripped you on purpose, that good-for-nothing bully!"

"Good thing there was a healer to repair the damage that he created. My name is Jarrod, by the way. Pleased to meet you."

"Healer? But don't your powers only work on living things?"

Jarrod shook his head.

"Our powers work to fix what is broken, be it a person or an object. Quite handy, don't you think?"

Elijah nodded, impressed. The boy sitting beside him introduced himself as Samuel, and the one beside him as Harry. Elijah found the boy sitting next to Adara – named Benjamin – particularly amusing, for he kept pulling faces at his stew and cracking ridiculous jokes.

Elijah fit effortlessly into the group's conversations, and soon found himself forgetting the strange altercation with Zachariah. It was almost as if it had never happened! Almost, had it not been for Adara.

"So why did Eldest Sapiens want you so desperately?" she inquired.

Elijah choked on his spoonful of rice. He looked up, meeting the expectant faces of his newly made friends. He didn't want to lie to them, but he couldn't tell them the truth either. Zachariah's arrival was bad news, and the frantic mentions of the Occidierumgave Elijah the impression that it was not a good topic to mention whilst eating a meal.

"Oh, it was nothing. He just wanted to make sure I was feeling better." Elijah averted his gaze as Adara narrowed her eyes. He felt strangely vulnerable under her calculating gaze. Seconds later, her eyes widened.

"So Surazal is your mentor! No wonder Sebastian hates you so much."

"I never said—"

"She didn't tell you?" Jarrod sputtered.

"Tell me what?"

He looked from Jarrod to Adara, noticing the unmistakeable glare she was giving him, as if to scare him into silence. But Jarrod took no notice.

"Her affinity. She's a telepath. A mind reader."

Adara banged her fists against the table and stood up in a violent rage. Without looking back, she stalked out of the room. At precisely that moment, the others at his table stood up and made their way to the doors. Elijah, who had gotten up to follow Adara after her outburst, was stopped by a hand on his shoulder. It belonged to Sebastian.

"Leave her alone. All you'll do is make her angrier and goodness knows what terror that abomination will unleash on us. Besides, you wouldn't want to get into trouble for wandering the corridors at night on your first day here, would you?" He smirked, clearly enjoying Elijah's discomfort.

Sebastian patted Elijah on the shoulder and walked off, taking his entourage of mean-looking boys with him. Elijah looked around for his friends, but failed to locate them. He figured Sebastian and his cronies had scared them off. Elijah waded through the sea of people and made his way to the doors. He was surrounded by people, yet had never felt so alone.

CHAPTER 11

ELIJAH FOLLOWED A group of boys down the now familiar passageway towards the residential areas. He tried making idle conversation, but the boys had no interest in him. Sighing internally, he made his way alone to his room.

As he approached the wooden door, he saw a lean, tall figure leaning against it. Surazal. He noticed Elijah approaching and straightened up, grinning.

"You made quite the impression in the dining hall today. I don't think I've ever seen a bowl of stew fly that high into the air in my life!" Elijah blushed and looked away.

"Never you mind. Accidents happen." Surazal waved a hand absentmindedly and went on, "Your schedule will be the same as everyone else's. Breakfast at seven, two hours of physical training with the rest of the boys, and then two hours of Potential, where you learn how to control your affinity. Sadly, you have a rare affinity. There is no specific Elder who can teach you to control your power, so you and a few others with rare affinities will be taught by Lucian. After lunch, you will have an hour of free time, after which your training schedule will be repeated. However, there is one exception for you; Instead of having physical training in the evening, you will be meeting with Eldest Sapiens. Understood?" Elijah blinked rapidly and nodded.

"I'd best be off; you have a visitor waiting inside your room. Goodnight." His catlike eyes gleaming, Surazal turned round, and with a swish of his robes, he walked swiftly away. Elijah watched the retreating figure of his mentor with a growing sense of unease. Something about his nonchalant demeanour seemed unusual, but Elijah couldn't put his finger on it.

Shrugging, he opened the door to his room. No sooner had he entered than a figure leapt off his bed and pounced at him.

"Elijah! Are you alright? Did Sebastian hurt you? I can help cure you, if you'd like." Jarrod flitted around, concerned, looking like the lankiest bird Elijah had ever laid his eyes on. All his annoyance disappeared, and he laughed.

"I'm quite unhurt, though it perhaps is a good idea that you don't disappear from my side and leave me alone with Sebastian and his cronies. You never know when I might need your power."

Jarrod smiled uneasily.

"Sorry about that. Sebastian scares me witless. Just the thought of him gives me the shivers!" He shuddered for effect, and Elijah nodded knowingly.

"We can help each other out, then? You can show me what life around here is like, and I could help you stand your ground against Sebastian."

Jarrod's face brightened, and they shook hands.

"Deal," he said. "I'd better get going. Although Brother Lucian isn't as bad as Surazal, he wouldn't tolerate me roaming the halls past curfew. See you tomorrow, Elijah."

Elijah shut the door behind Jarrod and made his way to the bed. He had made friends on his first day itself! *Not bad for a farmer's boy*, he thought. He removed his shoes and lay on the bed. He was so overwhelmed by his first day that he was sure sleep would elude him, but it seemed the excitement had sapped all his strength, and he fell sound asleep in moments.

*

Elijah fidgeted with the training gear he had donned. Over his shirt, he wore a vest of supple leather that, although soft under his fingers, would be able to withstand most blows his training was likely to involve. Hopefully. He wore black trousers of the same material that had loops that could hold weapons, but at present they held a single blunt staff of wood. Adara, as it turned out, was missing from class. Elijah wondered where she was.

"How can you stand to train in this?" Elijah grumbled. "It's uncomfortable, distractingly so. I can just imagine myself in a fight, still struggling with my gear while my enemy slashes me to ribbons. What a catastrophic mess I'd cause!" Jarrod, who stood beside him, chortled.

"It's not so bad. You'll get used to it. Besides, these pieces of wood can only do so much harm. I remember my first time in this gear. I nearly—"

A crash at the other end of the room made the whole class of twenty boys stop conversing and look up. Jarrod jumped mid-sentence, startled by the sudden cacophony. Surazal had kicked over a stand full of slender swords with wicked edges.

"Are you all done then? Permission to start with the training?" Sarcasm dripped from his words.

He strode straight into the heart of the room, and his hushed students formed a circle around him. Surazal took a fleeting look around the room, his gaze calculating as he sized up his batch of students. His gaze paused on Elijah, and his scowl deepened.

"For those who conveniently left their brains in an unknown corridor, this training session involves only physical training, so don't go panicking and use your affinity or teleport if your opponent is charging at you. If I do sense the usage of one's affinity," his gaze whipped toward Jarrod (whose affinity would give him the upper hand in a fight), "there will be severe consequences." The classwas mute, calculating what the consequences were likely to be. Apparently that wasn't the reaction he was expecting, and Surazal's golden eyes widened in mock shock.

"Heavens forbid, is it possible I have a more dim-witted batch than last year?" He sighed and shook his head with self-pity, as if the thought of teaching his students was the most inhuman of punishments. But then he straightened up and barked, "What are you all standing here for? Pick a partner and start sparring! Your muscles aren't going to warm themselves!"

Elijah turned to Jarrod with a question in his eyes, but before Jarrod could nod, Surazal interposed.

"Not you, Elijah. Since it's your first day at training, you'll spar with *me*."

Elijah looked from Surazal's beckoning fingers to Jarrod's startled face which changed into an expression of pity. He walked toward Surazal, who had a gleam in his golden eyes. He drew a similar piece of wood from his own weapons belt, except that it was whittled so finely as to be sharper than Elijah's.

Elijah gulped down his fear; he was looking into the face of a tiger, and all he had to defend himself was a wooden stick. Marvellous. The way his luck was going, he wouldn't leave this room without a few severed limbs at best.

Surazal settled into a stance, and Elijah mirrored him. He lifted up his staff, watching Surazal intently for a sign of motion, but none came. All around him, Elijah could hear the sound of wood clashing against wood as his companions sparred. Someone cried out in pain as his opponent's staff struck him, and Elijah looked around to discern the source of the shriek.

After it was too late, Elijah heard a whistling sound as something sailed through the air and hit him in the elbow. Hard. He jumped up with an indignant cry, his elbow stinging painfully, and whirled around to face Surazal, who was twirling his staff with a malicious smile on his face.

"Rule number one," he said, not pausing, "never take your eyes off your opponent."

Elijah rubbed his sore arm and grabbed his staff in both hands. He swung his staff towards Surazal, who sidestepped it easily and let his own staff lash out and catch Elijah at the knees. He staggered back, frustration making his nerve endings prickle.

Elijah's arms tensed as he brought them closer to his body to deliver his next blow. With a cry, he charged at Surazal and swung his staff with full force. But it cleaved cleanly through air. Surazal had ducked under the oncoming edge and emerged behind Elijah.

"Rule number two. Force is nothing without precision."

Elijah whipped around to face Surazal, who was now grinning with anticipation. His blood boiled and he began seeing red. The last time this had happened was before he attacked

Raven . . . Surazal's warning reverberated in his ears and Elijah forced himself to calm down, but to no avail. He lashed out again, aiming for Surazal's shoulder, but he easily blocked it with a counter strike. He aimed low, for his shin, but Surazal caught his staff on the edge of his own and pushed it back towards Elijah. They parried with each other, Surazal sidestepping potentially fatal blows with ease. Minutes turned into hours for the poor boy drenched in sweat. His arms felt like lead and his body hurt from the bruises Surazal was giving him, but Elijah managed to ascertain a pattern to his fighting style.

Surazal was letting Elijah strike first, which he would counter, and when Elijah withdrew from the attack, he'd swiftly land a blow to his body. Satisfied with his powers of deduction, Elijah tried to break the pattern by sidestepping straight after striking, thus avoiding Surazal's counter strike. But the veteran easily saw it coming, and thrust his staff out to rap Elijah sharply on the knuckles. The boy's staff slipped out of his hands, which were coated slick with sweat, and landed at the feet of another duo, which had finished its bout of sparring.

"Rule number three," chanted Surazal, "Expect the unexpected and deliver the same."

Rivulets of sweat ran down Elijah's brow and dripped into his shirt. He saw, chagrined, that Surazal hadn't even broken a sweat. In fact, he seemed rejuvenated and energised.

"Now," he called out, his cat-like eyes shimmering through his sparring-induced euphoria. "Who wants to go up against me next?"

*

"Are you sure you don't want me to heal you? The first training session is always the hardest. And it hurts the worst."

Jarrod didn't have to elaborate further. Elijah's arms hung limp at his sides like ten-tonne bricks. Every step he took sent spasms of pain up his body, but he declined the offer once again. He looked at his wrist, braceleted with bruises he had gained during the training, with pride. These were *his* scars, and he would let them fade away in their own time.

The boys walked towards the West Wing, where the Potential training rooms were situated. They parted ways when they reached a row of fifteen rooms, ranged down both sides of a long corridor. Elijah opened the doors and peeped into some. They were identical in size, but each was different in structure. Elijah saw a room full of lava, with only a few shifting pieces of bare rock, and he guessed that was for people with the affinity of fire. Similarly, there was a room full of plants and herbs and another one filled with orbs of watersuspended in the air.

"I go in here," Jarrod said, gesturing towards a room full of dusty, old books and broken urns filled with shrivelled plants. "You'll be in the room right opposite mine. See you after Potential."

Elijah waved, and winced as a shooting sensation of pain assaulted his shoulder. Gingerly, he brought his arm down. He turned around to enter his own training arena, but it was entirely the opposite of his expectations. Since this room catered to people with rare affinities, Elijah expected it to be a myriad of different terrains for each to practise his own affinity. But he was greeted by a bare room with a few people in chairs clustered in the centre of the room, facing a low platform. Elijah looked around for a familiar figure, and saw a startling mane of red hair in the front of the cluster. He looked around for an empty seat, and found two: one near Adara, and another near Sebastian, who sneered in an unwelcoming fashion. Elijah cursed inwardly, convinced that the fates were playing a cruel joke on him. He decided on the lesser of two evils, and strode to the front of the room, near Adara. As he passed by Sebastian, the older boy smirked and stuck his leg out, ready to catch Elijah unawares again.

But he had always been a fast learner.

Elijah stepped around his outstretched foot, and continued on his way. He sat down near Adara, his heart beating frantically. The last he had seen of her, she had looked positively murderous, a look he had only once before seen: on his mother, who was the singlemost short-tempered person he knew.

"Adara?" he said, nervous. In reply, she crossed her arms over her chest and turned away from him. "I really am sorry for keeping the contents of the meeting a secret from you, but I couldn't let everyone hear them!" Her scowl deepened, and she turned to face him.

"It's my fault. I shouldn't have been prying, nor should I have directed all my anger at you. I should go beat Jarrod to a pulp this instant, that stupid healer! He does more harm than good!"

"Would you ever have told me, had he not revealed your affinity?" Elijah enquired.

"Definitely! Just . . . after I got all the information I wanted from you. Curiosity is my besetting sin, after all." Elijah laughed, and Adara joined him in his laughter. They were friends again.

"I'm glad I have at least one familiar face in this session. I'll need someone to help me stay away from Sebastian."

"Oh, this is just temporary. I usually train with Sapiens," Adara said, not meeting his eyes.

But I thought I was the only one who had a session with Eldest, Elijah thought jealously.

A set of soft footfalls across the wooden floor of the room caused people to look up. Elder Lucian made his way towards the front of the room, smiling at the heads that swivelled his way.

"It seems we have a new face in our class this year, boys. And girl," he added, acknowledging Adara's presence. Elijah realised with a start that the only girl he had seen in the Brotherhood's underground sanctuary was Adara. All the other Invisitae were male.

"Now, as you know, you all have unique affinities that are uncommon in the Brotherhood of Invisitae. And it is my job, as Elder of *Infinitatem Potentialis*, to help you hone your affinities. Although my native affinity is healing, I'm sure I can help you with yours."

He scanned the room, his gaze falling on Sebastian.

"Ah, Sebastian! It's your last year of training isn't it?" Sebastian nodded smugly, basking in the attention from his fellow classmates. "Since you are on your way to becoming a fully-fledged Invisitus, why don't you demonstrate what Potential is supposed to help you achieve?"

Sebastian unfolded his tall, lean frame from his chair and confidently strode to stand beside Lucian.

His voice rang out:

"My affinity is metamorphosis, the ability to change my appearance at will. Let me demonstrate."

He shut his eyes momentarily, the orbs glazed silver when reopened. While the students watched with rapt attention, the silver faded from his eyes, giving way to deep cerulean irises. Elijah sat up straight in his seat; Sebastian's eyes looked nothing like their original green. A few seconds later, Sebastian's features began stretching and elongating. His hair began greying, complemented by wrinkles forming on his face. His knees began bending in on themselves as his legs shortened and chest broadened. Sebastian closed his eyes, his face contorted. The whole process looked excruciatingly painful, but Elijah's gaze was pinned on the spectacle unfolding in front of him.

There were gasps of incredulity in the crowd. Satisfied, Sebastian opened his eyes. But they were his no longer; Sebastian had morphed himself into a carbon copy of Elder Lucian, save for his clothes. Despite his aversion for the bully, Elijah had to admit that his affinity was impressive, to say the least.

Lucian clapped, delighted by the response the demonstration was getting.

"Anybody else want to showcase their abilities?" Several hands went up, Adara's included. Elijah's hand, though, sat firmly in his lap. Lucian looked disappointed at his lack of enthusiasm, but called on another boy called Marcus, whose affinity turned out to be manipulating time.

"That would have been handy this morning. He could have reversed time for me when I got out of bed late!" Elijah heard Sebastian say.

Over the course of the session, Elijah was introduced to the affinity of divination, flight, breathing underwater and emitting ultrasonic sounds. But the most spectacular by far was Adara's, all the more impressive as this was the first time the other pupils had shared a Potential class with her.

"I'm a mind-reader, a telepath. Nothing you ever think is going to slip past me, unless of course you put up a barrier, and only we telepaths know how to do that, too." They all laughed.

"For example, Elijah over here is worried sick that he'll faint after he demonstrates his affinity for us. That would be the third time in three days, wouldn't it?" Elijah's ears turned red as the class erupted into peals of laughter.

"But not only can I read minds, I can also do this," she said, levitating the empty chair next to Sebastian into the air. Sebastian gazed at it with wonder, until it came crashing down, missing his head by centimetres. He cried out indignantly, but Adara ignored him.

"And this." Suddenly Louis, a scrawny, owl-like boy with the power of divination stood up on his chair and waved his right hand. His shock was tangible as he reached out with his left hand to arrest the other's movement, until it too started swatting the air, useless under Adara's control.

"And with a little bit of trickery, I can make you question your very reality. After all, who needs metamorphosis when you have complete control of the human mind?" Adara grinned, her violet eyes bathed in flames of excitement. She looked Sebastian square in the eyes, and suddenly, her eyes changed to mirror his vivid green ones. The children watched, dumbstruck, as her features began to ripple and morph until Sebastian stood before them once more.

With a smug sigh, she let go of the illusion and flounced back to her seat, her disguise shattered like a sheet of glass. The children in the room looked bewildered, as if doused with a bucket of ice-cold water. Only Sebastian scowled and sank deeper into his seat.

Elijah sat transfixed, his mouth agape at her wonderful performance. Adara waved a hand in front of his face, and only then did he snap out of his reverie. She laughed at his bewildered expression and leaned in close.

"Your turn," she whispered.

Elijah stood up shakily and, as if of their own accord, his legs carried him to Lucian.

"My affinity – I can create storms," Elijah stammered. He tried to block out the awed murmurs of "Stormbringer" and will a current of wind into being. He couldn't even summon a light breeze. A finger of doubt ran down his spine. He looked desperately towards Lucian, who smiled reassuringly. He tried again, but to no avail. The whispers turned to titters, and Elijah's face heated with embarrassment. Some warrior he was. He couldn't consciously summon so much as a wisp of wind!

Elijah felt Adara's piercing stare on his person, and steeled his nerves, making one more attempt. Suddenly Elijah felt a tendril of wind blow past his ear. *Finally.* He just needed a little bit more . . .

Elijah felt his eyes glaze over, and his vision grew silver, as if a whisper-thin metal sheet had been placed in front of his eyes. He willed a current of air to propel him into the air, and the room filled with the collective gasp of his peers. Adrenaline coursed through his veins as he willed the winds to circle him like a tornado, lifting him up higher towards the ceiling.

He heard Lucian warning him to stop and come back down, but Elijah couldn't. The power sizzled through his veins. He could feel every individual drop of water suspended in the air around him. *Hurricane*, he thought, and the miniscule droplets rushed towards the funnel of wind around him.

Elijah heard a clap of thunder, followed by the sounds of rain falling in sheets, punctuated by the panicked screams of his comrades as they tried to protect themselves from the torrential downpour. Somebody cackled, and Elijah realised with a start that the sound had escaped from his own lips. He had done it! He'd created a veritable tempest underground, of all places!

Elijah felt ripe with power, the sheer energy of his affinity pooling into his fingertips. *His fingertips.* Elijah's heart sped up from fear rather than adrenaline. He felt the tell-tale crackle between his fingertips, and felt the translucent silver veil in his vision begin to thicken and turn opaque. He was slipping, losing himself to the power. *This couldn't be happening*, he thought, not here, *not now.* He willed the wind to die down and float him gently to the ground, but to no avail. The hurricane in the middle of which he was stuck refused to dissipate, and Elijah grew panicked. Without harnessing the hurricane, he would collapse the entire section of rock! Fractures appeared in the ceiling, and Elijah heard the others cry out, Lucian bellowing for them to get away from the boy and his raging squall.

Keep calm, Elijah. You're doing great. Elijah recoiled at the foreign presence in his mind. He recognised that voice . . .

Adara?

Yes. Listen to me and calm down. Don't let the power control you, for you control it.

But I've never managed consciously to control such a storm before. The last time, I barely knew what I was doing

– I only reined myself in because of Fabian. Why should this time be any different?

Because you don't hurt those who help you. Let me help you, Elijah.

Elijah felt Adara's consciousness brush against his own, soothing the fear he felt. A welcome numbness filled his head, and he sighed as he felt the heat in his palms ebb away.

Elijah felt his panic evaporate under Adara's influence, and slowly, gently he reined in the wind around him. He willed the column of wind to spiral him down, and he landed on the drenched stone floor. The cold travelled up through the soles of his shoes; the fire in his veins abated. The last of the wind dissipated, and Elijah's eyes returned to normalcy. He shuddered, and the momentarily suspended droplets of water crashed down onto the floor in a final, deafening deluge.

Elijah staggered back to his seat amidst a silence one commonly associates with death, acutely aware of the dumbfounded stares following him across the room. His knees buckled momentarily, and Lucian broke out of his reverie to steady him. Elijah waved his concern away and sat down looking straight ahead, his ears scarlet with embarrassment and worry.

He was contemplating getting irrevocably lost in the underground maze so as never to be found again, until someone clapped him hard on his shoulder. Elijah winced at the force of the gesture, and turned sharply when he heard a high-pitched laugh erupt from his aggressor. Rivulets of water streamed down her rosy cheeks from her sodden ringlets. Adara's eyes danced with mirth, and Elijah shuddered to think what went through her mind as she surveyed the sludgy carnage that he'd created.

"I was thinking," she supplied, "that we would make one hell of a team. And that I should keep an umbrella handy when I'm around you." She laughed again, her voice ringing through the stillness of the room.

"Thank you," Elijah said, his eyes sombre with sincerity.

Adara's eyes grew unexpectedly warm and she smiled softly.

"That's what friends are for, aren't they?"

CHAPTER 12

ELIJAH, JARROD AND Adara sat alone at the end of a lunch table, their meal finished. Most of the tables were now empty, and their friends too had headed off to wander about the corridors or take a much-needed nap. Jarrod was excitedly sharing the news of his training with his companions.

"And then, I blew on the shrivelled flower and it regained its colour!"

"I see why they call it 'the breath of life'," Adara said. Elijah opened his mouth to ask her how she knew the name of that particular action, but he remembered her spectacular telepathic abilities and kept his mouth shut.

"What did Elder Lucian make you do today?" Jarrod inquired.

"He had us showcase our affinities, since Elijah is a new student and all. You should see how he rides the wind. It's fantastic!" Adara said excitedly. He mentally sent a thank you her way, grateful for being spared the embarrassing retelling of his complete failure to harness the wind energy.

"Might I steal Elijah from you for a minute?" Fabian asked, having silently approached their table. Elijah excused himself, glad to see his companion once again. They walked some distance away from the table, near a wall by the door.

"I'm sorry I couldn't come see you sooner. I was held up with work for Eldest Sapiens."

"It's fine." Elijah waved a hand in dismissal. "I've been rather busy myself, what with training and all."

"So how does it feel? To finally be a part of your own kind?"

Elijah beamed, but his enthusiasm failed to reach his eyes.

"You still miss your mother, don't you?"

The boy nodded, blinking rapidly to diffuse the pressure of tears behind his eyes.

"It's alright to be homesick. When I first Turned, I missed my brother so much that I—"

Elijah looked up.

"What? You aren't a natural-born Invisitus?"

Fabian hissed, annoyed with himself.

"Though a huge majority of Invisitae are descendants from the original families that were turned by Penvellyn, I wasn't born an Invisitus like the rest of them here. I was Turned, like you. Though it was under a different set of circumstances."

"Fabian," Elijah questioned "What happened to your brother?"

Fabian shrugged off the question, but Elijah noticed the shift in his demeanour. Within seconds, he had withdrawn into himself, reliving momentsthat, by the look of it, pained Fabian to recollect.

"His body didn't accept the Change, that's all."

"I'm sorry for your loss." Elijah's concern was genuine.

But it seemed a dam had burst, and a suppressed torrent of words poured out of Fabian.

"He was always the stronger one, the one who could handle any amounts of pressure. And he was the one who wanted it most." Elijah didn't have to ask what "it" was. "I always thought that if anyone could withstand the Change, it would be he. And now he's—"

Fabian choked up, unable to continue. He drew raspy breaths, his head in his hands, and Elijah patted his shoulder nervously. After recovering, Fabian continued.

"We made the wrong choice, wanting to become Invisitae. I've given up so much because of it. In a moment, my life had changed."

He met Elijah's gaze with a scorching intensity.

"One wrong choice, one wrong step could make you lose everything. I learnt it the hard way, Elijah. You have to be wiser than that."

Fabian waved Elijah away, back to his friends, who were heading for the door. But just before Elijah went through Fabian called out again.

"Oh, and Elijah, heed my one piece of advice. Deception lurks everywhere. As the Stormbringer you need to know whom you can trust, for you never know which two-faced demon will betray you."

And on that merry note, Fabian sent off Elijah. He stayed slumped against the wall, trapped in his worst memories.

*

Fabian's heart constricted painfully as Elijah walked off, a bewildered look plastered on his face. Through immeasurable pain, he felt a twinge of guilt for laying such heavy truths on the shoulders of one so young, but in a world as cruel as theirs, there was no time for childlike ignorance.

Very few people had managed to become Invisitae without being born into an Invisitus family. Fabian, Elijah, Surazal, and even Zachariah were all birds of the same feather – they had been some of the few who had been Turned. Though Fabian had made the regrettable choice, and the others had been awarded no such luxury.

He clearly remembered the feeling of pride that graced his brother's face the day he perfected the tainted water. He had made just about enough for the two daggers, but the meagre yield was enough to bring a smile to his handsome face, a face that rarely smiled anymore.

He also remembered the confusion that had replaced it, when Eric's body began to reject the Change. Confusion that was soon replaced by anguish and a terrible expression of betrayal. As if it had been Fabian's fault that his body couldn't take the change.

"The power to move without obeying the laws of science, brother! Isn't that incredible?" Eric called out over his shoulder, still marvelling at the newly made vial of tainted water. "We'll be gods in this world, Fabian! I can just see it!"

Fabian smiled exuberantly, a shiver of excitement running down his spine. He also felt his excitement – tempered by a sense of foreboding – but he suppressed it. His brother had always been so closed off, that his declaration of the two of them as a single entity was enthralling. He would do anything to earn his brother's approval. Anything at all.

"Well, come on then. Give us the dagger," Eric called, his hand outstretched.

Fabian clutched the weapon to his breast. The dagger was a beautiful specimen, sapphire-hilted and carved with the most intricate of constellations. It bore an inscription meaning "Our paths are infinite", as his brother had told him once long ago. An inscription that suited the weapon's purpose completely – the purpose of creating Invisitae. The dagger was part of a pair, its sister being cradled by Eric. Fabian gently set the weapon in his brother's hand.

Eric had spent months poring over arcane texts and slaving over bubbling vials and tinctures, under Fabian's earnest gaze. But now, on the night of the culmination of their endeavours, Fabian could hardly reign in the fear roiling in the pit of his stomach.

He watched as his brother dipped the point of each dagger into the vial, the blades coming up thrumming with energy and pulsating with light. Eric handed his brother his dagger, and Fabian felt it flutter in his hand like a beating heart. He faced Eric, mirroring his brother's excited grin.

"Together?" Fabian called out, his voice tinged with fear.

"I wouldn't have it any other way," his brother replied reassuringly.

Fabian held the tip of dagger near the skin of his finger, his eyes unwavering as the pair held each other's gaze. Fabian drew the blade across his finger with a hiss, droplets of scarlet blood forming at the aperture. Almost instantly, threads of black laced themselves around his veins, making their way towards his heart.

Fabian cried out in alarm and pain as he sank to the ground, immobilised by the heat that brought rivulets of sweat to his brow and threatened to consume him. He writhed on the floor in pain as Eric watched with horrified interest.

"Fabian?" he called out worriedly. "What's happening to you? Are you rejecting the Change?"

Fabian gasped as he felt the ropes of black coil around his heart, and a light brighter than the sun blazing from his flushed skin.

When the light faded and his breathing slowed, Fabian looked around for his brother, finding him standing in the corner of the room, looking at his dagger in bewilderment.

"Eric," he croaked, "what's happening to me?"

His brother turned around, his expression souring. "You made it, brother,*" he spat the word out. "You're an Invisitus."*

Fabian's head was pounding too hard for him to feel excited.

"And—and you?"

This time, Eric turned around. By the light of the moon, Fabian could see his brother's eyes remained unchanged, the same startling green as his own were.

"Nothing."

Fabian swallowed, his eyes betraying the fear he felt at leaving his brother behind. But most of all, they showed the immeasurable pity for Eric. His brother, being as proud as he was, bared his teeth at Fabian. He stalked towards the heavily breathing man on the floor and grabbed him by the hair, ignoring the cries of pain emanating from Fabian. Eric drew his brother to his full height, Fabian's nose just centimetres below his older brother's.

"I. Don't. Want. Your. Pity," he spat, his eyes boring holes into Fabian's.

"I—I just—" Fabian began, trying to focus his blurry gaze.

"How fitting that the person who wanted, more than anything, to become an Invisitus has to watch his own brother be given that right. Even though the said brother had no idea whatsoever of the honour being bestowed upon him."

Fabian shrank away from Eric, each word assaulting him like a knife to the ribs.

"Look at me. Look at me!" *Eric cried, shaking his brother whose head lolled haplessly. Fabian was still feeling the effects of the Change.*

"I wanted this so badly. Of course I wouldn't get what I want. Poor Eric. I can never be the happy one. I can never have what I want. I should never have hoped that this time, my luck may have been different. It just goes to show how wanting never does anything."

Fabian let out a groan of pain, black spots dancing at the edge of his vision. He blinked a few times, and when his vision cleared, his heart clenched at the sight before him. Eric, his brave older brother, had tears in his eyes. Fabian tried to reach out to his brother, murmur soothing words to him as if he were a babe in arms, but his body was unresponsive.

"Those eyes could've been mine. They should've been mine. How dare you—" *Eric broke off with a gasp, his fingers loosening on the hair on Fabian's head. The younger boy slid to the ground unceremoniously, his head hitting the cold floor with a crack.*

He looked up, ignoring the groaning of the muscles in his neck, watching helplessly as his brother clawed at his own throat, as if fighting off an invisible arm that was choking him.

Eric sank to his knees, his pupils blown wide, green eyes rendered dark and black. Wetness flooded his cheeks as blood flowed out of his eyes, his mouth open in a wordless cry.

Fabian watched, horrified, as his brother began coughing up blood, features twisting with agony as he heaved. The bitter stench of bile burned Fabian's nostrils as he struggled to sit up, to scream, to do anything. *But he could only watch as his brother's body turned on itself, blood spurting out of every orifice, life draining out of every pore of his being. Fabian could only watch as Eric crumpled, a drained husk surrounded by a pool of scarlet.*

He lay there for a while, looking at the unmoving body of his brother, shell-shocked. This couldn't be happening, *he thought, his head pounding. He screamed his grief, his voice finally having come back to him, until his throat turned raw and his voice faded away like the brother he lost.*

CHAPTER 13

ELIJAH WALKED INTO Eldest's room, a cavernous area scattered with furniture. Tables and shelves were littered with antiques, glittering swords and sheaves of parchment. At the far end of the room was an elegant mahogany desk. He supposed he should go and wait there. On the wall near the door through which he had entered, hung a vast tapestry appearing to depict a story in a series of pictures: a man holding a vial of murky liquid in his hands, and another one of him consuming it, a glow engulfing his body. It dawned on Elijah that he had undergone the same thing; the tapestry depicted the Change. Elijah brushed his fingers against the soft cloth and continued on through the towering piles of thick volumes bound in fine leather and in cloth. He felt as if he was walking through a forest, the words trapped in the books whispering to him, tantalising him. He reached out to brush his fingertips against the fraying spine of a fabric-bound volume.

"What do you think of my humble abode? Do you like it?" a soft voice called out. Elijah drew his hand back. He nodded nervously, before realising with a start that the piles of books obscured him from the older man.

"Adara isn't the only telepath here, you know. So there's no use lying to me." His voice was one of mock-seriousness as he emerged from behind a teetering pile of books.

"It's . . . interesting."

"Quite so. I like to think of it as organised chaos. It reminds me of the constant battle of evil and good inside each and every one of us, *us* more than the average human."

Elijah shuffled his feet, uncertain as to how he should respond. Sapiens motioned towards a chair placed in front of his desk. Elijah went forward as Eldest took his place behind the desk. He patted a thick book that rested on the table, its supple leather spine hanging off an intricate web of string.

"Just a bit of light reading," he said, bright eyes twinkling with mirth.

"Now, I can understand that you are confused by your new life and have many questions. I'm here to help you find the answers."

Elijah took a deep breath, getting ready to reveal the questions pounding inside his head.

"Fabian explained to me what we are, several times, but I still don't understand how we came to be. How did we get here? *Why* are we here? And—"

Eldest bellowed with laughter, causing the piles of books to tremble worryingly.

"Fabian told me that you were inquisitive, but I didn't know just how seriously I had to heed his words!"

Elijah crossed and uncrossed his legs.

"Nonetheless, I shall do my best to answer all of your questions. The story of our creation was, to put it simply, an accident. We were created by an infamous alchemist, Robert Penvellyn. Like all alchemists at the time, Penvellyn was in search of the ultimate elixir, the elixir of life. However, it had a special significance for him, as the Welsh village he hailed from had been struck by a fearsome plague that threatened its existence.

"Penvellyn once worked in the royal court, but his fanatical quest made him fall out of favour, and he was exiled to his estate in the Welsh countryside where he continued his experiments in secret. He succeeded; not only that, he created a fountain of tainted water. Soon enough, Penvellyn too was affected by the plague, and out of desperation, he consumed the liquid he had created.

"Instead of simply curing him of his illness, or even giving him the secret to eternal life, it turned him into a supreme warrior with unnatural abilities. Penvellyn soon turned the rest of the affected villagers, and the Invisitae were born.

"Penvellyn had always been a philanthropist, and so he vowed to use his powers for good. You asked what we are here for, Elijah, and that answer is simple: We live in the shadows and protect the people from the unknown perils of the world. Thieves, murderers, hunger; we use our affinities and abilities to help those in need, and protect them from danger."

Elijah's eyes widened. He was just a boy; could he really handle such a responsibility?

Sapiens smiled kindly.

"Don't worry, Stormbringer. You are the strongest of us all. In time, you can handle anything."

"What about the dagger that changed me? What does that have to do with Penvellyn?" Elijah asked.

"Very little, in fact. The dagger that changed you was found at Fabian's side when we rescued him after he had been newly changed. He claims it has a twin, but it hasn't surfaced so far. Hopefully, it never will. There is little good that can happen should the dagger fall into the wrong hands."

"The original Invisitae, on the other hand, were created by ingesting the tainted water created by Penvellyn. The Fountain is preserved in this very labyrinth. Alas, I cannot tell you where exactly it is." He smiled at the flush that settled across Elijah's cheeks, betraying the nature of his unasked question.

"The only two people who know the location of the Fountain of tainted water are me, and my new apprentice.

So long as the tainted water in the Fountain runs, there will be no end to the line of the Invisitae. It is of the utmost importance to preserve the secret of its location, as the Fountain is the very source of our abilities."

"The thing about a change, Elijah, is there is always a way to reverse it. And the Fountain happens to be an integral ingredient in doing so. I believe the Occidierum have worked out a way to mix other ingredients with tainted water to make a potion that reverses the Change. But it is not known what the after-effects will be. Though the tainted water made the Invisitae, introduction of another dosage into the bloodstream – or anywhere on our bodies – would be dangerous. Fatal, even."

Eldest unfolded his arms and drew back his runed sleeve, exposing a penny-sized star-shaped burn below his elbow.

"This was what happened to me, when a drop from the Fountain grazed my flesh by accident, Elijah. Imagine the destruction the Occidierum could cause if they got hold of the water."

Elijah shuddered, and Sapiens covered his arm, once again hiding his scar from view.

"You've been through the Change, Elijah. Can you possibly imagine how painful the reversal of such a change would be?" Elijah blanched at the thought, phantom aches from the Change lingering in his bones.

"I don't think I could survive feeling like that again," Elijah said, solemnly. He fidgeted with the threads of his tunic. He remembered what little he'd overheard about the presence of a cure for their "condition", and he put two and two together. "That's what they want, isn't it? The location of the Fountain."

Sapiens seemed to age years in the seconds that passed, and he nodded slowly.

Elijah decided he would ask Adara to show him around the mansion, in hopes that they might discover the Fountain of tainted water.

"I wouldn't bother," Eldest said. "Barely a few even know it still exists, much less how to find it."

"And do the Occidierum know about it?"

Sapiens's expression soured. He paused and then continued with a sigh.

"Yes, they do. But only the Eldest of the Brotherhood is trusted with its true location, as I am and the Eldest before me was."

Elijah tapped his chin, deep in thought.

"Zachariah had said that he was being trained to be Eldest. Does that mean he knows where the Fountain of tainted water is?"

Sapiens's expression turned grave.

"Thankfully, no, he does not. There was a time several years ago when I believed that he was the one who should take my place as Eldest. Then – it would be shortly before you were born, in fact – he betrayed us all. He had been dabbling with the enemy, and had been corrupted by the Court with the promise of riches untold." Sapiens shuddered as he struggled to repress his memories – memories of a young boy once so pure of heart who lost out to his vices, a boy who betrayed his kin for the promise of a life of no hiding, no fear.

"Who are the Occidierum? Are they the ones Zachariah was working for?" Elijah asked, guilty for interrupting the Eldest's reverie.

"Although we work for the good of the people, they are often afraid of our capabilities. It is human nature to lash out due to fear, and that is exactly why the Occidierum exist. They are a group of assassins, so to speak, mercenaries paid by the Court to eradicate any people suspected of using magic and witchcraft."

Elijah's skin prickled with gooseflesh as a finger of fear ran down his spine.

"What court?" he asked. "Does the Queen hate us?" He was, of course, thinking of the Queen in London.

"No, no, not the British royal court. This is the Court of the Knights Templar," Sapiens clarified. "They claim to be descendants of the Knights Templar from the time of the Crusades, but that is doubtful. Even so, it doesn't make them any less dangerous. We might possess inhuman abilities, but we bleed just like any ordinary person. And die like them too. No ability we have can stop a blade from piercing our hearts."

"But why are they after me?"

"Zachariah may be a spineless traitor, but he is no liar. What he said was true. You are a bane for your enemies and a boon for your allies. Without the Stormbringer, we have no hope of survival. The Occidierum are getting stronger by the day, and somehow, they have begun adding people like us to their ranks." For a moment, Elijah glimpsed the crushing weight plaguing Sapiens. A weight that came with being the protector of a people whose very existence was being threatened. But in an instant, Sapiens regained his composure, making Elijah wonder if he had been imagining things. "Lucian told me about your inability to control your affinity." Elijah cringed inwardly, for it seemed the incident would forever haunt him.

Sapiens chuckled at his reaction and continued.

"It is mostly because you are still a fledgling. In fact, you shouldn't even be able to *use* your affinity; it has been such a short period of time since you Changed! However, it is also because the powers that surge within you are so strong that you find it hard to channel, and therefore, hard to control them."

"So you're saying that although I'm supposed to be the saviourof the Invisitae, I will be unable to control my own powers?"

"It will be a challenge, but it is not impossible. I have full faith that you will protect whoever needs you."

Elijah nodded, his mind reeling with the recent onslaught of information.

"Now that you know the truth, I will have to set up telepathic blocks in your mind. They are called wards. The wards will keep your thoughts inside your own head and, more importantly, keep *others* out of them. God forbid another mind reader read your thoughts!"

"They'd know all my weaknesses, find out how to target me."

"Exactly. Now, stay calm. This will only take a second."

Sapiens shut his eyes, exuding a sense of serenity. He placed his palms down on the table, his long fingers splayed across the wood. Elijah felt as if a door was being sealed in all four corners of his mind, creaking shut inch by inch. He began feeling closed off, secure, until he felt Sapiens's presence in his own mind. The sensation was so alien that Elijah's immediate reaction was panic and he began pulling away from the unfamiliar presence in his head. Sapiens tried to console him, but he couldn't stop fighting him. Suddenly Elijah felt numbness settle into his consciousness, his body going limp in the chair. Silent tears squeezed out of his tightly shut eyes, streaking down his face, cutting through the prickling chill on his skin. Minutes dragged on for hours, and after an infinity of breathlessness, it was over.

Sapiens looked up, apologetic.

"I must ask for your forgiveness for that. But I must say, you handled it a lot better than . . . others."

"I was just frightened, that's all. I had never experienced another consciousness right inside my head . . . Adara spoke to me in my mind, but she didn't enter; Zachariah almost came in. It seemed surreal, yet intrusive. I'm not entirely sure I enjoyed it. But if the wards work, I won't ever have to go through this again, will I?" Eldest nodded, relieved.

"I suggest you get back to your friends now. The others must have finished training, so I won't keep you any longer." Elijah rose up to leave, muttering his thanks.

"Though, Elijah," Sapiens, who had started reading through the book on his desk, said, "I don't think they'd need a telepath to read your thoughts." He looked up at the boy who stood silhouetted in the doorway, a sad smile playing upon his lips.

"One can see them all too clearly in your eyes."

CHAPTER 14

"AGAIN!"

Elijah groaned with frustration. He had been made to repeat the same manoeuvre on his fifth sack-cloth dummy for the hundredth time in the training session. All the others had sheared through several other practice targets and were on to tactics in one-on-one combat, while Surazal made Elijah constantly repeat the arduous task, but to no avail. They were armed with real swords today, but for all the good Elijah did with his, it might have been the wooden one of his first Physical Training class.

First he doesn't let me keep up with the other boys in training and then he complains that I'm left behind! Elijah thought for the thousandth time that week. He had begun mastering the power of wind in Potential, and had even begun to hold his own against Sebastian. The only thing he had trouble with was Physical Training or, more accurately, his instructor.

"Are you intentionally trying to make it hard for yourself, boy? Or are you just naturally incompetent?" Surazal taunted in his silky voice. "I've never seen anyone so defeated by an inanimate object, not even Fabian with a steel bolt. And believe me when I say that's a tough act to follow."

Elijah couldn't take it anymore. He was tired of being ridiculed by his so-called mentor, tired of being told that he wasn't worthy of the honour he had been conferred. He hacked away at the target in a last attempt at solace, muttering angrily under his breath all the while.

"Why can't he just leave me alone?" *Slash.*

"Can't he see that I'm trying my best?" *Hack.*

"I'm sick and tired of being the only one left behind."

Elijah landed one last blow and looked to see the damage he had inflicted. But the faceless body looked more like it had landed on a pile of blunt rocks and less like it had been sliced open by the wickedly sharp blade of a sword.

Elijah's vision turned red, his eyes narrowing in frustration and pent-up rage. Suddenly, his vision became sharper, more focused. Elijah could see every strand of string poking out of the sack, could feel the beads of perspiration streaming down his back and sticking his leathern vest to his body. With an innate sense of intuition, Elijah raised his blade above his head and brought it down on the dummy with a roar.

The sword cleaved through its target, slicing it into two symmetrical halves that fell to the ground with a thump. Jarrod, who was just a few feet away, stood agape at the spectacle in front of him.

"Elijah. You're—you're *glowing.*"

And indeed he was. Elijah's pale skin pulsed with a healthy bronze sheen, the tracery of blue veins throbbing as adrenaline coursed through them.

Elijah swerved towards Surazal, who had a satisfied smile on his face.

"That's more like it. You may even be ready to train with a real opponent now," Surazal admitted grudgingly.

Elijah's chest swelled with pride. *That's more like it.*

"After you practise on the next row of targets." *I spoke too soon,* Elijah thought, deflating.

Elijah heard tinkling laughter in his head. The response to his thought was so unexpected that he jumped. Surazal's eyes narrowed as he observed the boy. He pretended not to look and walked away, observing the other students and barking out periodic insults.

Not bad. For an amateur.

Adara.

How did you guess? Her voice dripped with sarcasm.

How'd you get through the wards in my mind?

I'm stronger than most telepaths. Besides, the wards are of no use if you voluntarily let me into your thoughts, Elijah. Though I wouldn't expect a novice like you to know that.

Novice, huh? I bet this novice *can take you in a fight.*

And what made you reach that conclusion?

Firstly, you are undeniably a girl.

Elijah felt Adara suppress her indignation as she thought, *Go on.*

Plus, you don't do physical training.

I may not do physical training with the lot of you, but that doesn't mean I don't train at all.

But you can't be very good then, if you have to train alone.

Or maybe they're just worried that you will all be winded ten seconds into a fight with me.

I highly doubt that, which is why I challenge you to a duel.

I accept your challenge. But just one thing, Elijah, don't place your bets yet.

Elijah felt her presence in his mind recede, as if he had just splashed his face with cold water.

"Are you done, then? We don't have all day!" Surazal called out from the far side of the room, beckoning Elijah over. "You'll spar with Harry today. Both of you are equally weak and incompetent in the art of hand-to-hand combat, so you'll both be fine."

Elijah and his opponent shifted into their stances and began circling each other. Neither wanted to land the first blow, so they circled each other for a long time. They would have continued to do so had somebody not impatiently cleared their throat behind them.

"I think you have the wrong room. I believe the ballet session is a little way down the hall." Sebastian. Elijah would have recognised the boy's smug, self-satisfied voice anywhere.

"I'd request you to kindly leave my pupils alone," said Surazal with cold indifference.

"But, Elder. They're just circling each other! What technique is that part of? Surely I could be of help." Sebastian's tone changed from a snotty peril's to that of an overeager schoolboy in the blink of an eye. Some other students even stifled a laugh at the sudden metamorphosis that was so characteristic to his behaviour in Surazal's presence.

"Very well. You can help Elijah train for the day."

Sebastian's face split into a wide grin, his euphoria at the attention from Surazal shining through his eyes.

Elijah, listen to me. The only thing Sebastian hates more than losing is losing in front of Surazal. He'll want to make sure that Surazal's eyes are on him and him alone. Use that to your advantage.

Understood, Elijah thought shakily.

Sebastian lunged, his blade a blur of silver as it came crashing towards Elijah's head. With a startled cry, he leapt aside. Sebastian stifled a laugh and Elijah's ears turned apple red.

Show no fear, Elijah! You're only as lethal as your opponent thinks you are.

Elijah steadied his beating heart and wiped his face clean of emotion. He advanced, his blade drawn. By now, Sebastian had resumed his customary stance of calculated carelessness and was twirling his weapon around. *I'll wipe that insolent smile off his face*, Elijah gritted his teeth and brought his weapon down on his opponent in a frontal arc, which Sebastian sidestepped easily.

"Come on, is that the best you can do?" Sebastian taunted, evoking titters from the onlookers. Sebastian swivelled to gauge Surazal's reaction but found his gaze fixed on his charge. Sebastian'snostrils flared with annoyance and he charged, sweeping his sword in a horizontal arc, which Elijah met head-on with his sword. Sparks flew as the two blades collided, and Elijah felt the sword wobble in his opponent's hands. He looked up into the cold eyes that pierced his own, and underneath the façade of nonchalance, he saw burning envy.

His anger makes him unstable, so—

Yes, I gathered that, thank you. Elijah snapped inwardly. *I don't have to be a telepath to see that.*

Elijah thought he heard Adara grumbling in his mind, but before he could concentrate on it, Sebastian struck again.

Sebastian attacked relentlessly, and it took all of Elijah's concentration to keep him from being slaughtered. They danced in a frenzy of slashes and strikes, a lethal game on lithe feet. Elijah would have been battered beyond repair ages ago, had it not been for Adara's voice in his head noticing shifts in Sebastian's demeanour before he even registered them.

See how his right eye twitches? He does that when he gets nervous. And the sag of his right shoulder is an indication of his fatigue. He can't keep up his attacks for much longer.

Sebastian lunged once more at Elijah, his eyes turned towards Surazal, and Elijah jumped at his chance. He ducked away from Sebastian's blade and dropping to one knee, he struck the back of his opponent's knees with the flat of his sword-blade. With a cry, Sebastian crumpled to the ground.

Elijah felt a momentary spike of triumph at his victory, but it fizzled out when he saw the murderous gleam in the boy's eyes.

"You cheating *pig!*" Sebastian said, storming towards Elijah. A hush fell over the room as the older boy lifted Elijah up by the collar. "The girl was helping you, wasn't she? Tell me the truth or I'll skin you alive. TELL ME!"

Elijah looked squarely into Sebastian's eyes. For the first time, it occurred to him that the boy might not be entirely sane.

"That's enough, boys." Elijah felt Sebastian momentarily stiffen at the sound of Surazal's voice, and then loosen his grip. "Unconventional method, Elijah. But then again, what can we expect from Heaven's own warrior?"

"Next time, Sebastian, let's try keeping our eyes on the opponent and not the audience. How does that sound?"

Sebastian turned a violent shade of red, his features contorting as he tried to suppress the colouring before it was noticed. But to no avail.

"Let's get back to training. We've wasted enough time as it is."

Elijah felt exhilarated, adrenaline coursing through his veins and making his nerve endings sizzle. The world seemed . . . sharper, more focused. Elijah made his way towards a gob-smacked Jarrod, who gazed at him in awe.

"Blimey, where did you learn to fight like that?"

"Oh, around and about," Elijah smirked.

"So is it true, then? Was Adara really helping you out?" Jarrod leaned in and lowered his voice.

Elijah nodded, still beaming at his good fortune.

"Elijah, I'd like to have a word with you. In private," Surazal called out over his shoulder, as he walked off to his desk.

Elijah gulped and walked over to his mentor. Surazal watched with a bemused expression, but his eyes were alert.

"I must say, your tactics were quite unexpected. Nonetheless, they were effective. And that leads me to believe you had help during your fight."

"You suspect foul play because I *won*? Have you such little faith in my abilities?" Elijah sputtered.

Surazal chuckled, but his golden eyes remained devoid of laughter.

"Let's not get ahead of ourselves. All I'm saying is Sebastian is one of our brightest, most skilled initiates. And you are just a fledgling, a novice. No amount of beginner's luck could have made you win that fight."

Elijah looked at his feet, shamed at being reprimanded. He looked up again upon feeling a hand on his shoulder.

"You need to learn how to fight for yourself. You will not always find help, and I don't want you to get hurt because there is no one to watch your back. Threats are always out there, lad. You never know when someone might strike."

The words were delivered with such a deliberate sincerity, they almost seemed forced. But Elijah did not have time to mull them over, for no more than a second later, a matron ran into the room shrieking.

"The Occidierum are here! Hide the children! They're—"

A horrible squelch of a blade piercing flesh was heard, and the woman's features went slack. She sank to the ground, eyes wide and unstaring, her last scream forever etched upon her face. There was a moment of utter silence, and then all hell broke loose.

CHAPTER 16

PANICKED SCREAMS PIERCED the air and bounced off the cavernous walls. Sections of the wall parted and formed doorways to passages. Children ran helter-skelter, their fear enunciated in their silvered eyes. The braver ones stood with their swords drawn, hiding their fear behind a cracked mask of vigilance, while the others pushed and shoved each other in order to make it to the numerous passageways that had sprung up in the walls.

Surazal strode around the room barking out orders, guiding the young Invisitae into the passages.

"Follow the passageways. They lead straight to the sanctuaries!" he cried out.

Elijah. Sapiens's voice boomed in his skull, drowning out the frantic cries. *You must not be discovered. Have Sebastian escort you to my quarters. It is the only place safe enough for you.*

Elijah scoured the room for his adversary and found him making his way towards Elijah.

"Come on," Sebastian said tersely. His looked tense, with no sign of the hatred of a few moments ago. He strode on further and ran his hands along the stone wall until he found a loose fragment. Sebastian nudged the stone deeper into its socket and, much to Elijah's surprise, the shards around it began undulating and receding. They seemed to be forming an ordinary passageway, but Elijah knew better.

Sebastian turned around, motioning for Elijah to follow him. Elijah took one last sweeping glance around the room and stepped into the corridor. The hole in the wall behind them folded in on itself, obscuring the panic from view.

"Hurry up!" Sebastian hissed. Not for the first time, Elijah wondered whether trusting Sebastian was indeed the wisest course of action. But before he could ponder that, the older boy grabbed his arm and began running.

Sebastian navigated the bends and curves of the passage with the sureness of a veteran, Elijah trailing behind him. His heart thumped wildly against his chest as it tried to keep up with his frantic footfalls. They passed by several branching passageways which carried ominous echoes to Elijah's ears. Once, he thought he heard the scuffle of boots against the stone floor and swerved around to ascertain the source but his eyes met an empty passageway. Wait, he thought, was that a *cat*?

A rough hand on his shoulder jarred him back to the present, and the weight of what he'd done settled on him.

"What were you thinking, stopping like that? You'll get us both killed!" Sebastian hissed.

"I thought I saw—"

"NO TIME FOR THAT!"

He has an uncanny ability to scream softly, Elijah thought. They hastened, and soon came upon a fork in the underground passageway. Sebastian sped up.

"Go left!" he said. "Don't stop for anything or anyone. As much as I hate to say this, you getting caught could be disastrous for us, so you must make haste."

As he spoke, his eyes seemed to melt and his form rippled dizzyingly. Elijah watched Sebastian with a queasy feeling in his stomach, but he couldn't look away. With a start, he realised Sebastian was turning into an exact replica of him.

"Don't just stand there! You're not *that* much of a looker!" the other boy said, when he took in Elijah's vacant expression. Then, with a laugh eerily like his own, Sebastian took off down the right corridor.

Elijah took the other passage, eyes flicking frantically, too afraid to stop even though his lungs burned from exertion. Sharp wheezing breaths escaped his lips and the muscles in his slender legs screamed with indignation as he ploughed forwards.

Elijah, duck!

Elijah felt his legs give way of their own accord, and landed squarely on his knees, the impact rattling his teeth in their sockets. He tried to get up, but his knees were cemented to the ground. As soon as he hit the ground, he felt something fly over his head, skimming the tips of his unruly hair. *An arrow!*

The compulsion having abandoned his limbs, Elijah scrambled back to his feet and ran faster than ever, keeping to the shadows cast by the walls of the tunnel, his heartbeat drowning out the footfalls of his assailant. He had to run, he had to escape, he—

Elijah's nose connected with sinewy flesh, which, he would soon realise, belonged to the arm of Sven, Sapiens's personal guard.

"Move aside, boy," Sven growled in his bass voice, thrusting Elijah behind him, engulfing his face completely with his humongous hands. Elijah wiped the grime off his face, grateful for a chance to rest behind his hulking, muscular shelter.

"There's someone behind me! I thought I was fast enough, but I wasn't and if it hadn't been for that voice I'd never have evaded his arrows," Elijah rattled on in his relief, stopping only when Sven placed a thick finger on his lips, silencing him.

"Let *me* do the talking, son," he said.

Turning his back to Elijah, Sven took a deep breath, his chest expanding in an almost comical manner. Elijah watched, mute, as Sven unleashed the air from his lungs in the form of a deafeningly shrill scream that drained the blood from the boy's face. He tried to drown out the sound by clamping his palms over his ears, but the shriek was all-pervading.

"Easy there, Sven. I think my ears might fall off!"

A familiar voice cried out over the uproar. But Sven was too caught up in his scream to notice. Surazal ran into his line of sight, grimacing as he tried – and failed – to protect his ears from the assault.

Elijah suppressed a snort of laughter as Sven's great bearded jaws clamped shut instantaneously. The hulking man blinked stupidly at Elijah's mentor.

"What of the assailant?" he asked, his voice back to its normal baritone.

"Disposed of," Surazal replied, looking quizzically in Elijah's direction. "Why are you still here? You were instructed to go to Sapiens!"

Elijah stepped back.

"I—I stumbled."

"Over flat ground?"

Elijah hoped the dim lighting hid his blush as he nodded in the affirmative.

Surazal shook his head and strode forward, and taking hold of Elijah's arm, pushed him at Sven.

"The worst is over, but you're not safe yet. They're still inside, therefore you must hide with Sapiens and Shrilly here." Pretending not to notice Sven's withering glare in his direction, he continued, "Get going now, hurry it up." He swung about and walked swiftly back the way he had come.

"Who is still inside?" Elijah demanded, following Sven away from Surazal's retreating figure.

"The Occidierum have infiltrated the Manor. So Zachariah truly has betrayed us," Sven muttered, a brief scowl marring his features.

Elijah followed Sven into Sapiens's room, nearly running into his companion's stiff back when he stopped abruptly.

"Sven? What's wrong?" Elijah inquired, his voice fading to a whisper as he stepped out from behind the man and took in the scene in front of him.

Books lay scattered everywhere. Pages ripped apart from the invaluable tomes, tossed around like chaff. Elijah hissed through his teeth. He had never had many books, but his mother had taught him that a book is more than just the weight of its pages.

Elijah's gaze roamed around the room, resting on the slumped figure of Sapiens behind his ornate wooden desk. The old man had buried his face in his palms, obscuring it from vision, but Elijah could sense the frustration and despair rolling off him in swathes, making the atmosphere bitter.

Without looking up, Sapiens said, with a forced upbeat clip to his voice,

"Nothing to worry about, Sven. I'll take it from here. Go ensure the rest of the children are safe."

Sven bowed, his massive brows creased with concern.

"Azriel and Jacob have secured your quarters, and the children should all have reached the Sanctuary," he said. "I shall help defend on the frontlines." With one last look at Elijah through hooded eyes, the man vanished.

Having regained his composure, Sapiens folded his hands and regarded Elijah.

"Now then, Elijah. I was hoping our next meeting would be under more favourable circumstances." A weak smile accompanied his words.

"Shouldn't we fight, too?" Elijah asked, quashing the feeling of panic that rose up within him. "I'm the Stormbringer, I'm the saviour! I—"

"You are entirely too young and too precious to risk. Besides, you don't even know how to teleport unassisted. When fighting against the Occidierum, our nimbleness is our greatest asset. No human can keep up with someone who has infinite paths at their disposal."

"What about you?" Elijah thought back to the stories of valiant leaders and kings his mother had so fondly told him. In those, the leader was always at the front lines, mesmerising in their effortless strength and charisma. The leader sitting before him was nothing but a weary old man.

"Ah, Elijah. There are some secrets that are too precious to be lost, therefore making the people that keep them even more so."

There appeared nothing more to be said or done. Elijah resigned himself to waiting in idleness, while goodness knew what was happening all over the Manor.

He then spent an eternity leafing through Sapiens's tomes in studied silence, running his hands over the script in the parchment, stroking the pages where the ink bled into them. He looked up every so often, when an Invisitus appeared outside the doorway and came in frantically to deliver news to their leader. It seems, Elijah thought to himself after Sven had reappeared outside the doorway for the second time, as though one required Sapiens's permission to be in his room. Even though the frantic Invisitae had no problem teleporting out of it, they could not teleport in.

After approximately an hour of deliberate silence, Surazal and another Elder ("Ah! Brother Edmund!" Sapiens had exclaimed upon seeing the slight, bespectacled man) swept into the room, announcing that the intruders had been dispatched, and that the passages were free to roam once again.

"Were there any casualties?" Sapiens asked, worry and relief warring in his eyes.

Surazal shook his head.

"We lost Matron Sandrine, may peace be with her. However, the children are safe, and the worst of the injuries was a stab in the lung suffered by Morrissey. Brother Lucian is working on him, though, so you needn't worry."

"I will confirm whether you are correct in the assumption that we are truly rid of the enemy," Sapiens said, closing his eyes and assuming a meditative stance. The briefest expression of exasperation flit over Surazal's face, so fast that Elijah almost missed it.

In a few seconds, Sapiens opened his silver-etched eyes.

"I can sense no alien consciousnesses," he said. "Very well, instruct the matrons to release the children from the Sanctuary."

"Eldest . . ." Edmund, who had been silent so far said, "We faced a slight problem while engaged in combat with the Occidierum."

Elijah craned his ears.

"It was hardly a problem, Brother. Think nothing of it," Surazal said, his arrogance colouring his voice with impatience.

"But it was! My group of offensive telepaths and I couldn't use our attacks against several of the intruders. They all wore these masks . . . we couldn't penetrate them. We have no way of knowing how many of them were there, or if any got away."

"Good thing my fighters were present. This is why, Eldest, it is always wiser to trust your brawn, and not the arcane arts to tackle a problem," Surazal said.

Elijah heard a soft crackle, like moist wood burning, and felt a prickle go up his neck. He looked up, noticing Surazal jump away from Edmund with a yelp and fall silent.

Edmund smiled sardonically.

"Speak when spoken to, *Brother.*"

Sapiens stood up, straightening to his full, impressive height. Energy pulsated around him threateningly, and the bickering twosome fell immediately silent.

"I may be old, but I have not gone soft. You would do well to remember the situation we are in, Brothers. Fighting amongst ourselves will accomplish nothing.

"We need the power of fist and mind in equal measure, and if you are unable to lead your squadrons due to petty disagreements . . ."

Elijah swallowed, chastising himself for believing for even a second that Sapiens was a senile old man. Sapiens sensed the growing smell of fear emanating from Elijah, and backed off, his point made.

"What mask do you speak of?" Sapiens continued, addressing Edmund.

"Judging by the fact that Fabian had no effect on them, I'd say they're steel masks. Just like the rest of their weapons. It makes sense, as your defensive telepaths couldn't sense their presences before they struck either."

"If they are steel, I would not have been able to sense their presence either. There might still be some Occidierum in the mansion," Sapiens mused, brow furrowing.

"Eldest, no need to worry. I, myself, have checked the labyrinth. It's clear. No Occidierum hiding there, I'm certain of it." Surazal said with conviction.

Sapiens looked deep in thought, and Surazal walked over to Elijah. He gestured for the boy to replace the book, and called him to join the adults in their conversation.

"Alright there?" he whispered as they made their way back to Edmund and Sapiens. Elijah nodded.

"Sapiens, if it is alright with you, I would like to take my charge aside for a while, I have important things to tell him," Surazal requested.

Sapiens waved them off with a smile in Elijah's direction.

"Be careful, Elijah," Edmund prompted, looking doubtfully at Surazal. Surazal bared his teeth at Edmund by way of retaliation, looking undoubtedly feline, like a lion poised for attack.

"That warning is redundant now, isn't it? Seeing as the enemy has been disposed of."

Edmund looked Surazal straight in the eyes, his gaze unflinching, and whispered,

"The enemy is everywhere."

CHAPTER 16

ELIJAH FOLLOWED SURAZAL out of Sapiens's quarters, the chill from Edmund's whispers still seeping through his bones and sending shivers down his spine.

Surazal scoffed without turning around.

"That Edmund – what a joke."

"I take it there's bad blood between the two of you?" Elijah pried.

"I'll say. He thinks less of me, because I am not a natural-born Invisitus. I was Turned, like you." Elijah's eyebrows shot up in silent surprise. Just how many people had been Turned?

Surazal turned to face Elijah abruptly, the rune-patterned sleeves of his robe swaying as if prompted by an invisible wind.

"Though the Occidierum have been removed from the Manor, it doesn't mean you are entirely safe. Edmund may be a good-for-nothing lunatic, but was right about one thing: the enemy *is* everywhere."

"You're the Stormbringer," he smirked, as if privy to a private joke, "so you have to be twice as careful. I want you to head to your room *now*. Don't utter a word to anyone on your way there."

Elijah felt his neck prickle with irritation. He was his mother's son, and he hated to be told what to do. Surazal scrutinised Elijah's face with his mesmerising gold eyes, the bright silver accentuating the darker flecks of tan in his irises. Elijah nodded, knowing full well he wouldn't obey.

Satisfied with his reaction, Surazal nodded once.

"Best be off, then," he said.

Elijah turned and walked down the corridor, and broke into a run after turning the corner. He had been fully aware that Surazal had been watching him, and wanted nothing more than to put as much distance as possible between them.

Elijah ran blindly, trying to shake off the unnerving feeling of Surazal's gaze burning holes into his back. He spotted Jarrod and Adarastanding a little way down the corridor, their backs to him, whispering intently together. He slowed to a brisk stride, feeling immediately better around his friends.

"What brings you here?" he inquired. The two children jumped with shock, their conversation interrupted.

"Elijah! Wow, you don't look so good. We wanted to make sure you wouldn't lose your way, and perhaps show you around a bit, but that can wait, I guess," Jarrod said, making his way towards the boy.

"Don't worry about me, I'm fine. I'd love to see the Manor!" Elijah reassured his friends.

Jarrod patted him good-naturedly on the back and led the way.

"Adara and I know all the nooks and crannies of this place. One day with us, and you'll be an expert at navigating the pathways too!"

"Well, what are you waiting for?" Adara grabbed Elijah's hand and dragged him along, pausing momentarily to throw a concerned glance at the boy.

The trio made their way down a corridor, chatting amicably. Jarrod and Adara, who had never been outside the labyrinth since they were brought there, peppered Elijah with questions of the outside world and in turn, Elijah asked them about their – and now, his – world.

"What is the Stormbringer supposed to do?" Elijah asked, "They say I'm the Stormbringer, but I can hardly do anything!"

"The Stormbringer is Heaven's Warrior. Sapiens says he's the saviour of our people, the Chosen One who will succeed Robert Penvellyn and become the leader of the Invisitae." Adara supplied, proudly flaunting the extra attention she got from Sapiens.

Not to be outdone, Elijah said,

"Sapiens also said something about the Occidierum? That they're here to kill us?"

Adara and Jarrod shivered in unison.

"I've only seen their kind once," Jarrod said. "When I was first brought here. My father was killed by one of them. They're supposed to be human, but they've got no humanity left. Killing people left, right and centre. Adara's entire family was wiped out by them."

Elijah looked at Adara sympathetically.

"I—I'm sorry. It couldn't have been easy growing up without your family, could it?"

"Enough of that! It's my turn to ask the questions now." Elijah got the feeling she was avoiding answering, but didn't press it; Adara was frightening when angered. "You lived on a *farm?*" Adara's eyes widened, "I've only ever seen memories of farms. It must have been *incredible!* Did you have a cow?" she punctuated her words with exuberant hand gestures, looking at Elijah expectantly.

"We did, once. Margie, her name was. But we had to sell her off for money to buy food," Elijah said. The memory of his cow was bittersweet.

"Couldn't you just grow some food?" Jarrod asked.

"We've been having a drought in Iowa. It is so hot and dry, you can hardly grow much of anything on the farm. Even the weeds don't survive," Elijah informed them.

"Maybe I could help! One day, when we get out of here, I'll heal the farm with my *breath of life*! And we can meet your mother, too! She sounds wonderful. A lot like Matron

Alma. She and the other matrons are the closest thing to mothers that we have here," Jarrod said, laughing as he saw Adara wince at the comparison.

Elijah was overwhelmed with emotion. His friends wanted to help him and his mother.

"That—that would be wonderful, thank you. Except, I don't know *when* I'll meet her. If at all." He sniffed and blinked furiously to quell the formation of tears in his eyes.

Abruptly, Adara turned around to face Elijah and poked him smartly in the ribs.

"OW! What was that for?" he bellowed, rubbing his stinging skin.

"Sorry, I never know how to deal with such strong emotion," she said, wringing her hands shamefacedly. The two boys looked at her incredulously, and promptly burst into laughter.

Jarrod wiped tears of laughter from his eyes and said,

"You can sift through people's minds but can't process their emotions?" Adara stared warningly at the boy, but he was too overcome at the incredulity of his revelation to notice her murderous glare.

Elijah sobered up enough to notice her angry expression.

"But you're a *girl*. Mother says girls are more in touch with their emotions," he said mildly.

Adara sputtered and then regained her composure.

"You're a *boy*. Sapiens says boys are better at physical combat, but we both know that's a lie in your case. Some Stormbringer you'll make."

Elijah felt pinpricks of anger pepper his skin.

"I can beat you any day."

"Prove it." Adara stepped up to Elijah menacingly.

Wisps of wind began tearing at Elijah's clothes and pulling at his hair, the intense energy manifesting itself into his affinity. Pebbles and dirt rose off the floor, being pulled into the mini tornado forming at the boy's feet. Adara seemed unperturbed by his personal gale, as her own telekinetic abilities were involuntarily causing her long tendrils of hair to rise up around her head like a halo. The atmosphere was pregnant with the combined energy of the two young Invisitae, causing the very walls of the passage to shudder.

"Adara, do you hear something?" Jarrod teetered nervously, eyes flitting around the passage and taking in the rumbling sounds of protest the walls of the passage were emitting.

"Elijah, we shouldn't be here. I—I sense something moving in the passage," Jarrod called out again. But his friend was too preoccupied with avoiding the murderous young girl to care about unknown presences. Breathing the power-saturated air made Elijah feel giddy, and raised the hair on the nape of his neck.

She glared pointedly at Jarrod through silver, unseeing eyes, and he was flung back, ramming into the wall of the passage with a yelp. Jarrod stood up and backed away from the girl. Elijah glanced at Jarrod, distracted by his cry.

He stumbled suddenly, his feet giving way under him. With a startled squeak, he realised that his momentary lapse in attention had given Adara the upper hand. She stalked towards him with a predatory grace, blinding in her awe-inspiring power. Elijah quaked with fear as Adara came closer . . . closer . . .

A cry of pure, unadulterated terror pierced the air. Elijah and Adara swivelled to look at Jarrod, only to see him babbling incoherently and pointing at something behind them. Adara's eyes took on their normal, violet hue.

"Jarrod? What are you looking at?" she asked.

"Adara, duck!" Elijah yelled, having spun round in the direction Jarrod was pointing and noticed the figure concealing itself in the shadows behind her. Just then, the figure launched a blade at Adara, but she swerved, the blade missing its mark by a hair's breadth. It sailed over Elijah's head, but he used his command over wind to send it ricocheting back to its wielder. The children heard a cry of pain, and the muffled sounds of a person running away.

"They're still in the mansion . . ." Elijah gulped.

Adara's eyes shone mirthlessly.

"What good is a patrol team if they don't check for *stragglers*?"

"We have to teleport to Sapiens! Tell him we're under siege!" Jarrod cried, grabbing his friends by their shoulders. Adara threw his arm off her shoulder, eyes smouldering.

"You can run all you want, Jarrod, but I refuse to."

Jarrod's eyes grew wide with exasperation.

"Adara, they're the *Occidierum*! They'll kill you!"

"They killed my parents!" she cried, her words speaking volumes of anguish. She pushed the two boys together. "Just let me handle this one. I know I can."

Adara raced off into the dimly lit corridor, the two boys looking worriedly after the rapidly diminishing echoes of her footsteps.

CHAPTER 17

ELIJAH GRABBED JARROD'S shoulders in a frenzy, and hoisted the boy to his feet.

"She's mad, she is. I'm going after her, you go and get Sapiens. And *hurry!*"

Jarrod nodded, steeling his wide-eyed gaze into a mask that betrayed none of the anxiety Elijah knew he harboured inside.

Elijah patted his friend on the shoulder and took off running, commanding the air around him into a gale to help propel him forward. Elijah faintly heard Jarrod say, "Be careful!" over the deafening roar of wind in his ear, but when he looked back for a millisecond, the boy was gone.

Revved up with the adrenaline coursing through his veins, Elijah raced down the corridor taken by Adara, forcing himself to swallow down the feeling of dread that rose up like bile in his throat.

*

Within the Brotherhood, Adara was famed for very many things: being the only female Invisitus, being notorious for her illusory powers and even the special bond between Sapiens and her. However, she was perhaps the most well-known for her impulsive decisions and headfirst hurtles into dangerous situations.

She raced after the retreating footsteps of the assassin, trying desperately to close the gap between her and her prey. But the assassin had faster, more long-legged strides than the young girl, and it infuriated her not to be able to catch up to him.

She opened her mind, probing the passageways for the man's consciousness. In her mind's eye, she could see the map of the underground labyrinth, and could even sense the presences of the people in the tunnels close by. She waded through the consciousnesses she recognised, looking for the alien one belonging to the assassin. But as she was sifting through them, she felt a single consciousness reach out to her so fervently, it made her head throb. *Elijah.*

She tried to push him away and resume her search, but the insistent pulsing of his consciousness made it impossible. Without slowing her pace, she barked, *What is it?*

The relief her friend felt was tangible through their connected consciousnesses. *Good. You're safe. Angry Adara equals safe Adara.*

A flush stained her cheeks, either from exertion or silent happiness, and she snorted to mask the smile playing upon her lips. In just the few days they had known each other, Elijah had noticed several things about her that she had barely paid attention to herself. He had wormed his way through her defences, and it was infuriating, but she had to admit she'd been flattered.

Adara, I'm coming after you. You can't possibly take down one of the Occidierum on your own!

Adara's expression darkened, and she lost all pleasant thoughts aimed for the boy. *I can, too. I've trained for so much longer than you have, and I'm not just a child. Don't come after me, I want to take this man down myself.*

She felt his mind flutter with obvious frustration. *Adara, please listen. The Elders are on their way, you don't have to do this by yourself, let them handle it.*

Images flashed through Adara's head, memories of the gore and bloodshed that manifested themselves as now-expected nightmares. She channelled the memories to her friend, memories of a little girl that was undeniably Adara crying bloody murder as she tugged at the sleeve of a headless man – her father –who lay in a pool of crimson blood, the colour of her own flaming hair. Adara felt Elijah shudder as she showed him the image of the Occidierum assassins tying her mother to the door of her own house and setting her alight, the flaming, shrieking body of her mother sending plumes of acrid smoke into the air as she thrashed wildly, trying to protect herself from the tongues of fire that lapped at her, peeling the singed skin off her melting bones. *For allying with practitioners of witchcraft,* she'd heard the killers say as they watched the flames dance across the wooden walls of the house, walls that would soon be reduced to glowing embers.

She hated them, hated the people that had slaughtered her family. And she *would* have her revenge. *You see, Elijah,* she said with a steely tang to her voice, *I do.*

Without a smidgen of hesitation, he replied, *Then I'm coming with you.*

The ice around her heart chipped, and she considered relenting, but stopped herself. *You can't, Elijah. This is something I have to do myself. Besides, I can handle one assassin. Nothing will happen to me, I promise.*

She felt the fight rise up in his throat, but she blocked him out of her head, severing the connection once and for all.

Without her concentration centred on her mental conversation with Elijah, Adara felt as if she had been doused with a pail of ice water. Her gaze cleared, and she began searching the area with her mind once again.

Almost too late, Adara felt a shift in the air, and instantly became aware of an unfamiliar consciousness up ahead of her. She found herself caught in a dead-end, devoid of opportunity to escape. Fabian had always taught her not to turn her back on her enemy, and she couldn't escape without doing so.

"Well, well. Who's come to play?" She heard a cold baritone voice echoing, sheathed in the darkness of the cavern walls just a few feet away from her. She backed away slowly, trying to put as much distance between her and the voice as possible.

Simultaneously, a man stepped out from the shadows. He was tall, with glittering dark eyes, a stark contrast to his fair hair – so ashen, it looked as if it had been leached of colour. The man's arms were thickly corded with muscles that shifted under the sleeves of his red tunic as he made his way towards her. *Like writhing snakes,*Adara thought, disgusted. He looked like he could take on even Surazal in a fistfight, but she was certain he had no hope against a telepathic Invisitus.

Just one assassin. She could dispatch him easily.

The odds were in her favour.

Reading the look of triumph on her face, the man laughed a soft, chiding laugh. As if he was laughing at a child who had toppled over while walking on unsteady feet. Somehow, this laugh made Adara's blood grow cold.

Her eyes adjusted to the poorly-lit cavern, and she could make out two more figures waiting silently in the shadows. With a wordless gesture from the raven-eyed man, the figures stepped out to stand beside him.

A man and a woman, dressed in tunics of grey, stood with their arms folded. They wore identical half-masks of a feline aspect, perhaps of the lions Adara had read so much about in Sapiens's books. With a languid motion, they brought the masks off their faces, revealing sharp, cruel eyes the colour of ditch-water, emphasised by their pallor and the ruthless smiles etched on their lips. Instantaneously, Adara could sense their consciousnesses flicker into existence, every bit as guarded as the fair-haired man.

"Steel," she whispered, and the man in the middle gave her a cheeky grin that didn't meet his eyes.

"Guilty," he said, and the Terrible Twins sniggered, as if he had made the funniest joke they'd heard.

Everything made sense now. Every Invisitus had a weakness for steel. It seemed to inhibit them from using their affinity, and not even Fabian,- who had control of most metals, could manipulate it. *The steel masks must have hidden their consciousnesses from me*, she thought.

Three assassins. Adara swallowed.

The tables had turned.

*

The minute Adara severed their connection, Elijah felt dread seep into the pit of his stomach. He could sense that she was in trouble, and had an inkling that by the time Jarrod got here with the Elders, it would be too late.

His lungs burned with exhaustion, but the nutritious food and rigorous training he received under the Brotherhood's care had cultivated muscles, albeit small ones, on Elijah's lithe legs. Ignoring the stitch in his side, he propelled forwards, softly calling on the power of wind to aid him.

As if responding to his urgency, the wind around him began whipping at his breeches, slowly turning into a swirling hurricane that lightly lifted Elijah off his feet. The winds surged under his feet, asking for release of their true potential and threatening to overtake Elijah's control over them, but the novice Invisitus checked the invisible reins he had on the wind, and they died down from a roaring hurricane to a silent yet swift gale.

This is what it feels like to be in control and completely free, Elijah thought, adrenaline coursing through his veins like liquid fire. He almost laughed out loud with exhilaration, but he had a feeling it would be counterproductive and would only put him and Adara in further danger.

With his new surge of speed, he sped through the winding corridor with silent ease, his brow glistening with concentration-induced sweat from whenever the wind under his control tried to break free.

Soon, he came close enough to hear the sounds of a conversation.

". . . never get me. He'll come for me, I know it," he heard Adara growl, her feral tone masking the fear she felt.

"The *Stormbringer*? He is not the Stormbringer. He is but a child." Elijah heard an alien voice croon, slimy as the underbelly of the garden snakes he often saw during the summer months.

Elijah hovered behind a bulge in the wall of the cavern, taking in the scene in front of him.

Adarawas kneeling on the rocky floor, her tunic riddled with cuts, as if attacked by a pair of shears. Red liquid oozed from a few wounds, dripping off her glistening skin and onto the ground, which devoured it hungrily. Her chest heaved with exertion, and Elijah watched as she writhed, trying to free her arms from the vice-like grip of two almost-identically dressed people with their backs to Elijah.

The speaker, a tall and oddly coloured man, bent his frame to Adara's height and gripped her chin with his impossibly long fingers. Elijah gritted his teeth. The man turned Adara's head towards him with little visible effort, and leered at her, eyes wide.

Adara, for her part, spat a mouthful of blood at his face, and the man recoiled with an angered shriek. The vibrant crimson was startling against the pallor of his skin.

"You little rat! I'll slit your feisty little throat, Lazarus be damned!" His voice lost all traces of his previous silken calm, and the hatred he felt leapt unbound.

Lazarus, Elijah thought. He'd heard that name before.

The man made his way to Adara, something metallic glinting in his hands. *A knife!* Elijah's vision reddened, his anger and fear for Adara loosening the control he had over the wind keeping him afloat. The wind broke free of its shackles and roared deafeningly. The four people, unaware of his presence, looked up, momentarily distracted.

"Who's there?" the man asked. Elijah felt a wave of relief wash over him as Adara joined her consciousness to his. Elijah used the control he had over the long-suppressed wind to propel it towards his friend's captors. He roared in unison with the wind as it surged against the bewildered captors, throwing them off their now unsteady feet. Elijah felt a silver sheen coat his vision, but this time, he didn't feel out of control. This time, the sheen helped him clear his head of all the emotional clutter and fear he harboured, making him focus on just the task at hand. He could feel the incredible energy the air was charged with, purring at him like an obedient housecat. This time, he wouldn't be overpowered by the element he called his own.

This time, he was in control.

Elijah raised his arms, gesturing towards the fair-haired man, and the wind around him increased intensity of its wild gusting. The man cried out in bewilderment as he was buffeted by the wind on all sides, the blows just as potent as if being delivered by a person.

Elijah cocked his head towards the two who had Adara caught in between them, and commanded the wind to hoist them up into the air. They were flung violently into the air, Adara wrenched from their grasp. He watched as Adara got unsteadily to her feet in the midst of the strong gale, her eyes turning solid silver.

Leave them to me, he heard her say in his mind.

Elijah nodded imperceptibly and relinquished the hold the wind had on them. He smirked as the two fell like rocks, shrieking madly.

Adara let the two fall for a short distance and, just before they hit the ground, she stopped their fall by stilling the atmosphere around them. During Elijah's wind-blowing frenzy, the masks had been knocked clean off their faces, and they were now prime targets for her. She watched as the woman blinked dazedly and fell face-first, unconscious. Adara turned her attention away from the woman, and set to reversing the wards put on the man's mind. It was a complicated process as the wards were incredibly strong, undeniably the work of Zachariah. But Adara was stronger, and she made quick work of it. Soon, she would be in his mind, and could help Elijah take on the other man.

Meanwhile, Elijah had ceased his attacks on the man, and had instead pinned him to a cavern wall. Elijah used his control over the air to thin the atmosphere around the man, making it more and more difficult for him to breathe. The fair-haired man's breathing grew laboured and raspy, and he clawed at his throat, his previously calculative eyes now simmering with hatred and fear. Elijah knew he should stop, that if he didn't the man would cease breathing altogether, but he was blinded by the agony he had heard in Adara's voice. Surely people who murdered without cause didn't deserve to live?

But if he took the life of the man now, would he be any better?

The man scrabbled at his throat with one hand, and blindly lashed out with his free hand, his fingernails gouging grooves into Elijah's cheek. Elijah hissed with indignation, and felt a surge of electricity course through his being. His heart fluttered with panic; summoning lightning at such close quarters was too much of a risk, especially with his mercurial control over it.

Elijah attempted to smother the surges of power, and in the bargain his control over the wind slackened. Seizing his chance, the man jumped at the vulnerable Elijah, something glinting in his hand. He hit Elijah hard enough to leave him winded, and the two of them fell to the ground. Elijah cried out in pain as he felt something wickedly sharp break through the skin of his exposed neck, and felt something blisteringly cold enter his skin through the puncture. Elijah scrabbled weakly at the man's tunic, trying to find purchase as the foreign substance made its way through Elijah's body, numbing his limbs and inducing a feeling of confused lucidity.

Through blurry vision, Elijah saw the man grin malevolently, the corners of his lips tweaking upwards.

"Liquefied steel," he said.

Elijah flashed back to Fabian's panicked expression when he had been restrained by the steel chains in the barn back home. He gurgled incoherently, and the man smacked him on the side of his head, his sneer never faltering.

"Not so valiant now, are we?"

The man stood up and brushed the dust off his breeches. He looked over at Adara, his smile faltering now. Elijah followed his gaze with his own unsteady one.

He didn't know whether it was the after-effect of the steel in his body, but Adara looked radiant. Her tunic was torn and dusty, and her hair was matted as she grappled with the now conscious woman Occidierum and her comrade, but her ivory skin glowed an ethereal silver, as if it was light pulsing through her veins instead of blood.

Adara feinted as the man lumbered towards her, and jabbed her foot forward so fast that Elijah thought lightning was flashing in the cavern. She moved like a hurricane, beautiful and devastating, as she fought with the two assassins, a seasoned veteran.

I was a fool to think I could take her on, he thought lucidly.

He watched her hair as she performed yet another feint-jab, fire wreathing her face and licking the tops of her shoulder. Elijah tried to reach out, as if to touch the trailing flames that fascinated him so, but his arms were unresponsive.

The man cursed audibly, and stepped back, melting into the shadows. With practised stealth, he silently made his way behind Adara, who stood breathing heavily over the unconscious body of the man at her feet, her violet eyes issuing a wordless challenge to the still-standing female assassin who gazed at her with bated breath. Elijah saw it coming too late.

The man crept up behind Adara, his arm drawn back, tense as a whip, brandishing the syringe he had used on Elijah.

Elijah screamed incoherently, and the girl spun to look at him with startled eyes.

You turned . . . your back to them! Elijah screamed in his mind groggily. Recognition dawned on her, but it was much too late.

The man brought his arm down in a swift arc, just as Adara swerved. But she was too slow, and the silver needle of the syringe bit into the skin of her shoulder.

The snake had found its mark.

Adara's red lips parted in a silent scream, and she fell to her knees, the light surrounding her diminishing abruptly.

Elijah felt himself crumple into the darkness.

*

"... Need to get her back *now!* There's so much at stake."

The urgency of the words made Elijah's eyes flutter, but when he tried to pry open his eyelids, he found himself unable to do so.

"We should send the boy, seeing as it's his fault."

Elijah could make out the steely voice of Surazal, dripping with contempt. Contempt for *him.*

Elijah cracked his eyes open slightly, and peered around. He was in a lamp-lit cavern, apparently part of the Manor's labyrinth. Before him stood a few Elders of the Brotherhood, of whom Elijah could recognise Lucian and Surazal. Sapiens stood in the corner of the cavern, eyes shut and hands folded as if in prayer, Fabian pacing the length of the cavern with relentless energy.

"Oh, thank goodness you're awake!" A slightly blurry and terribly anxious face loomed into his vision, shortly followed by a clammy hand to Elijah's forehead. It was Jarrod. "I was sure my healing spells weren't effective."

Elijah tried to form words with his mouth, but settled for a weak smile when his jaw refused to cooperate.

"He couldn't have known, he is not a seer. If it's anyone's fault, it's the girl's. She's always been too spirited for her own good," yet another seethed.

"How *dare* you blame the Bellator!" another defended.

Silence!

The word rang through as clear as the toll of a bell, and Elijah felt a certain compulsion to do exactly as commanded. Sapiens's order resounded in the abrupt lull in the cavern, despite the fact that he had uttered nothing.

Finally, Sapiens opened his eyes. They held the silver sheen that Elijah had now come to relate with a usage of one's affinity, but after it faded away Elijah was shocked to see the weariness within them.

"Today is a grave day indeed, but blaming one another will do nothing to aid the Bellator. For years we have protected this secret, nevertheless our enemies have got wind of it. It is undeniable, my brothers, that there is another traitor amongst us." His statement was punctuated by incredulous whispers and resigned sighs from the surrounding Elders.

"We must recover the Bellator, she is our only hope."

Elijah tried to sit up, making use of Jarrod and the cavern wall for support.

"Pardon me," he said, "but what exactly is this 'Bellator' business?"

The Elders swivelled round in unison, as if they had forgotten the children were even present.

Sapiens opened his mouth as if to speak, but was stopped by Surazal laying a deterring hand on his shoulder. Ignoring him, Sapiens went on.

"Well, I suppose you have the right to know, seeing as you are already thoroughly entwined with this."

He paused and took a shuddering breath, as if steeling himself for what he was about to say.

"Sir Robert Penvellyn, our founder, was perhaps the most gifted of all Invisitae. The tainted water blessed him with the ability to navigate the nebulous future, and this ability manifested itself in the form of a prophecy. Our people have always lived in danger, and he predicted that the dangers for our kind would only grow. After all, human beings are seldom tolerant of that which is different.

"But there is always a silver lining to every cloud, and this prophecy was no different. He predicted the coming of a saviour, whose power was limitless. The very winds would bow to his command." With this, Sapiens smiled at Elijah, whose eyes bulged. "Yes, my boy. As the Stormbringer, you are the warrior of our people, the saviour of our race.

"But," he continued, "there is one other that wields a power more magnificent than the Stormbringer. It is a person who bewitches the mind, who has potential that surpasses even Penvellyn's by tenfold, a person whose sole purpose is to unite Invisitae and humans and put an end to our suffering once and for all. The Bellator, the Hand of Heaven – the future of our people, our Protector.

"Few knew about the Bellator, save for Penvellyn and his trusted circle of Elders, and as the years passed and none with the desired affinities showed up, the prophecy was eventually forgotten. Until now, when both the Stormbringer and the Bellator – the Warrior as well as the Protector – were found."

Jarrod gasped behind him, a shocked "It can't be" escaping his lips. Meanwhile, Elijah's steel-addled brain struggled to make sense of the information Sapiens was giving him. Looking at his confusion, Surazal rolled his eyes impatiently.

"Heavens above, you imbecile! When will you understand?" he said, striding over and jerking Elijah to his feet.

"The reason this disappearance is so important – the secret we've been trying to protect is really a person," Lucian supplemented, his eyes betraying tenderness.

"It is she, Elijah." Elijah's head whipped around to face Fabian where he sagged onto the cavern walls, face unreadable as it was wreathed in shadows.

"The Bellator. It's Adara."

CHAPTER 18

ELIJAH FELT THE cold weight of realisation settle on his shoulders.

"So you pretended that I was the strongest Invisitus to protect Adara's identity?" he flashed his eyes around the room, but the Elders studiously avoided his gaze. "You *used* me."

Instantaneously, Fabian's head snapped up and he regarded Elijah with wide eyes.

"We would *never* use you, Elijah. We simply, in a manner of speaking, altered the truth."

"Are they not one and the same?" Jarrod whispered, finally out of his stupor.

Elijah heard an exasperated sigh emanate from Surazal.

"Enough is enough, boy. We shan't explain ourselves to you – all you need to know is that it was for the greater good."

Elijah bristled, and felt agitated currents of wind nip at his heels.

"Now, my brothers, we can't just stand here and let those bastard Occidierum get further away with the girl. We must save her, we must save ourselves." Surazal paused and surveyed the room. "Sapiens, in dire times like these I think it is only wise to turn to our strongest combatants." While speaking, he strode over to the Eldest and knelt before him, head bowed.

"*Servio tibi,*" he said. *I am yours to command.*

"Rise, warrior!" Sapiens boomed, lightly touching his shoulder. "I accept your offer, braveheart. But these are dark times, and I cannot burden your shoulders alone with such a grave responsibility, for it would lay a burden upon my conscience as well.

"Which is why I propose you be accompanied by yet another skilled warrior – Fabian." Elijah saw the fight flash in Surazal's eyes, but it disguised itself as resigned contempt in an instant. "A warrior is nothing without his metal, and the metal will not wield itself. Go forth, my brethren, bring our daughter of the heavens back."

"Very well, Eldest." Fabian turned to Surazal. "Gather your things, Brother. We will leave at first light."

With that, the men turned on their heels and disappeared. Elijah looked bewildered at Sapiens, but the older man only sighed and averted his gaze. Suddenly, cold fingers circled his wrist. Jarrod tugged at his arm. With the onslaught of information, Elijah had almost forgotten the presence of his friend.

"Elijah. I must talk to you *immediately*." Jarrod's voice quivered with urgency as he pulled Elijah out of the cave by the sleeve of his tunic. Elijah blinked worriedly. This was highly unlike Jarrod's otherwise calm demeanour.

He wrenched his arm away.

"What's the matter with *you*, Jarrod?"

Jarrod stopped and turned to face Elijah.

"Adara is our friend. We're going to find her too."

"But we're only children!" Elijah sputtered. "We can hardly be of help!"

"Invisitae are never *just children*, Elijah. We don't have that luxury. I've lived underground under the thumb of fear for too long. I won't bear any more of it, especially not without Adara."

Elijah stared at his friend. He spoke with such conviction that the silver in his brown eyes began to glow softly, like embers in the fire Marian would light during winter. His sallow skin took on a sun-kissed glow, as if anticipating the promise of the great outdoors.

"I've seen you fight, Elijah. You can protect us, no trouble. And I, in turn, will protect you. Lucian says he rarely meets healers as competent as me." Elijah could hear the pulse of a beating heart all around him, as if Jarrod's very words were alive.

"So? What do you say?" Jarrod asked, eyes dancing with anticipation.

Elijah nodded curtly, but before Elijah could speak, a voice spoke.

"My, my Jarrod, if that isn't the best idea you've ever come across." Elijah's blood froze.

"Sebastian." Jarrod's voice dripped with ice.

Laughing, the older boy stepped out of the shadows.

"You won't tell, will you?" Elijah said.

"Why ever should I not?" Sebastian sneered.

"If you do, I swear I'll—"

"Swear you'll do *what?* Blow air at my face?" He barked with laughter at his gibe.

Elijah willed the air near his palm to form a frigid current, and curled his fingers around it as if it were a whip. He flicked his wrist, directing the whip towards Sebastian's leg, and curling its end round his leg. The older boy cried out in alarm as he was swung into the air, upside down.

Elijah saw Sebastian's eyes gleam molten and in a second, he had turned into a spitting image of Adara. His leg was now too slender for the whip of air to hold, and he dropped gracefully down, twisting as he fell and landing on his toes like a cat.

While changing back into himself, Sebastian said,

"You'll have to do better than that to try and best me," he smirked, a gruesome sight on his amorphous features.

"What do you want, Sebastian?" Jarrod said.

"It's simple, you pansy," he said, now fully returned to his original form. "I want you to take me with you."

CHAPTER 19

FABIAN KNEW THAT sleep was important. He knew that adequate sleep could save his life in battle. But he *also* knew that there was little chance of him getting any this night.

For weeks he had been plagued by the nightmare of seeing his brother perish before his eyes. It haunted his dreams and pervaded his waking hours, like a semblance of movement caught in the corner of his eye; it made him feel watched. The dream etched itself into his face in the form of lines on his forehead, feeding off the healthy glow of his skin until it held the pallor of a corpse.

Fabian did not know why this nightmare had resurfaced, after so many years of its absence, but he'd begun dreading sleep once again.

However, this night was inherently different: he dreamt not of Eric, but of Adara.

In his dream, he saw her on the back of a burly male, who was flanked by a wiry man and the slender form of a woman. They marched in silence, even their footsteps were muffled. She was blindfolded and her arms were slack, but Fabian could tell that she was cognisant; though her limbs were deadened, her brain was no longer addled by the steel.

He looked around him; on his left-hand side, he saw acres and acres of grassland, populated by the coarse bristles he could feel through his breeches. To his right, a wide expanse of blue sea reigned. The waves leapt and crashed against the side of the cliff like ruthless falcons of the tide. Grey stone houses rose up in the distance like jagged teeth, marring the endless monotony of the grasslands. He recognised this place, from a long-forgotten excursion to the country taken with his family, back when they were still a family: Castlemartin.

Yes, he recognised it all, save for one detail.

Behind the village loomed a large, grey building. In the heat of the morning, the building looked smudged, an ink stain on the untarnished fabric of the sky. The alien unexpectedness of the building offended his eyes, and he resented it at once for marring one of the only fond memories of his childhood.

He followed the group of travellers, and the closer he got to the building the more sluggish he felt. A heavy metallic taste coated his tongue, resembling that of iron, but it seemed *other*. As if it were tainted. As if it were steel.

The building the group was headed for was made of steel.

Suddenly it dawned on him that this was not a dream, but a warning. The bitter taste of panic overwhelmed him as his consciousness joined with the bringer of the warning. He could sense her fear, sense the sluggish thrum of blood through her veins as it fought against the metallic poison coursing through them.

They would reach the stronghold in a few hours. This would be the last they'd hear from Adara.

Wake up, he heard her say. Fabian shuddered awake. He was breathing hard, as if he had been running for miles. An odd mixture of relief and dread settled in the pit of his stomach, slowing his heartbeat and clearing his mind.

Sis fortis, he thought. *Be brave. We will find you.*

CHAPTER 20

"ELIJAH! ELIJAH, WAKE up!"

Elijah rolled over in his sleep, mumbling,

"A few minutes, Mother."

A snigger ensued, and suddenly Elijah felt icy cold water hit his face. He sputtered indignantly and wiped the liquid from his squinted eyes.

A boyish laugh filled the room, and Elijah opened his eyes to see a red-faced Jarrod and a disdainful Sebastian standing at the foot of his bed.

"What time is it?" he asked, rubbing the last traces of sleep from his eyes.

"Time to get a move on. Pansy here overheard Fabian telling Elder Surazal about a dream he had, about Adara. He said something about Castlemartin – that's where we're headed," Sebastian said.

"But I've not got any weapons, nor any armour," Elijah said, bewildered, looking at his companions' protective gear and the scabbards strapped to their waists.

"That's alright, I've got you covered. I stole the storeroom's key from Elder Lucian last night; he always gets a bit silly after having his 'medicinal' sherry." Jarrod smirked knowingly, handing Elijah a sturdy jerkin, breeches, as well as a tough breastplate and shoulder braces.

Elijah undressed and put on the gear, surprised to find that it fit him rather well.

"They were too big," Jarrod supplied, "So I had Sebastian alter them slightly. He's rather handy with a needle, it seems."

Sebastian whipped out his sword from its scabbard and pointed it mock-threateningly at Jarrod.

"Needles aren't the only things I'm good at wielding, so you'd best keep that information to yourself, you hear me?" Jarrod and Elijah overlooked his threatening stance, and caught a glimpse of his reddened ears. Sharing a look, they launched into hysterics.

"What're you lot on about?" Sebastian said exasperated. "This is hardly a time for jokes!"

Elijah smothered his laughter.

"I'm so nervous right now that it's all I can do to distract myself," he confessed.

"Look at you, having a good laugh while your friend is undergoing God knows what at the mercy of the Occidierum. They could've thrown her off a cliff by now, but by all means, enjoy your little jokes," Sebastian said, icily.

That sobered the younger boys up completely. Elijah narrowed his eyes in confusion.

"Did you say cliffs?"

"As a matter of fact, I did. He mentioned a stronghold at the cliffs of Castlemartin."

Elijah blanched, remembering his nightmare, of Adara falling off the cliff. Could it be . . .?

"How are we getting there? None of us know what the place looks like," Jarrod said.

Elijah swallowed and spoke around the thick lump forming in his throat,

"I think I do."

Sensing his discomfort, Jarrod looked at him worriedly.

"Do you think you can teleport us all? You've never done something like this before . . ."

"I have no choice," Elijah interrupted. "If I am the Stormbringer, it is my duty to protect my people, and saving the Bellator is the main part of doing just that. I will do it. I *must*."

He reached his hands out to his companions, and they gripped his hands in theirs, solidarity in the face of fear.

"Are you ready?" he asked. His companions nodded the affirmative.

Elijah took a deep breath and steeled his nerves. He closed his eyes, picturing with great clarity the cliff, the sea, the craggy rocks and clumps of grass.

Vias nostras infinitam, he thought. *Take me to where I must go.*

He felt a pulling sensation in his gut, and suddenly he lost all sensation except for his friends beside him and his mind thrumming with one goal: saving Adara.

CHAPTER 21

TO ELIJAH, TELEPORTATION felt like a fever-induced haze. His body prickled with sensations and he was assaulted with fragmented images like shards of broken glass. The sounds of the places he passed by melded together to form a roar as deafening as that of the sea. It was all rather overwhelming, to be honest.

Which is why it was no surprise that he teetered backwards upon landing, tripping over a clump of roots and sending his companions sprawling along with him. The trio landed in a tangle of flailing limbs behind an overturned cart.

"Is everyone alright?" Elijah sat up, gingerly feeling a sore spot on his shoulder.

Jarrod groaned an affirmative as he straightened to peer over the wood blocking his vision. Sebastian blew grit off his lips, seething. His murderous expression made Elijah's breath quicken, and he felt the wind respond to his agitation, blowing wisps of his dark hair off his face in the concerned, fretting fashion of a mother.

"Stormbringer or not, I swear to *God*—" Sebastian's words were muffled by Jarrod crouching down and placing a palm on his lips, fingers shivering with fear.

"How dare you—" Sebastian began again, but Elijah silenced him by flicking sand at him through an almost untraceable gust of briny air.

In the sudden hush, the boys could discern the sounds of a scuffle. The clashing of swords could be heard, accompanied by the sound of laboured breathing.

"It's them," Jarrod whispered, voice shaking. "Surazal and Fabian – the Occidierum found them."

Elijah peeped out from behind the wooden cart shaft, regarding the scene with increasing fear. Diagonally to his right, he saw a group of six men whirling like dervishes, their swords indiscernible save for metallic clanging and a silver flash here and there. Sometimes, he thought he caught a flash of Surazal's rune-patterned armour, but as soon as he saw the spidery scrawl, it would vanish in an onslaught of attacks. A little further ahead, he saw Fabian with silvered eyes, surrounded by what at first glance seemed to be a storm cloud, but upon further inspection turned out to be tiny, wickedly sharp pieces of metal. The metal protected him as he grappled with six adversaries of his own, a menacing cocoon that protected his exposed flank from the other fighters while he engaged with one.

"This is madness," Elijah whispered. "Twelve against two? They can't last for much longer, can they?"

Sebastian flapped his hands agitatedly, motioning for Elijah to keep quiet. His gaze was trained where Elijah presumed Surazal was fighting, his eyes glowing with wonder as he watched with rapt attention. Elijah remembered the reverence Sebastian had for Surazal, and followed the direction of his gaze.

At first, he couldn't make out the form of his mentor because of the blinding, silvery glare of the sun gleaming off swords.

"Can you see him?" Elijah whispered.

"He's *all* you can see. Look for the light," Sebastian replied through gritted teeth.

He shielded his eyes from the glare, but the silver glints still obscured his vision. Then it dawned on him – the luminous silver glints *were* Surazal.

As he watched, the silver glints began taking a humanoid shape, a luminescent outline of a man who moved with unparalleled grace. Elijah could see the other men tiring, but Surazal's eerie silver-gold eyes showed no sign of fatigue.

Elijah watched, mesmerised, as Surazal disarmed a man with the point of his sword, and jabbed one behind him with the hilt in the same motion. Both men sank to the ground, unconscious, andSurazal bared his teeth as his halo grew brighter.

"That's his greatest strength," Sebastian whispered reverently. "The more opponents he defeats, the stronger he becomes."

Elijah watched with mute fascination as Surazal slashed at the back of his assailant's knee while avoiding the blow of another. He fought like he was dancing, Elijah realised, a thought reinforced by the almost feral smile playing upon Surazal's lips as two more of his enemies fell at the hand of his blade.

For a moment, Elijah drew his gaze towards Fabian, just in time to see him thrust his arm towards his last standing opponent with a cry and unleash the metal barbs at him, peppering his skin with spots of blood. His eyes returned to their piercing green as he relinquished control of the barbs, his incapacitated opponent falling to the ground. Fabian wiped sweat and blood off his face, chest heaving with exhaustion. His tunic stuck to his muscled chest where he'd been cut, and Elijah spied a deep gash on his arm that was turning a violent shade of green. Fabian subconsciously drew his free hand to the wound, and he winced.

"He's been poisoned!" Jarrod whispered urgently, "He'll need to be healed, and quickly!"

Ignoring the pain, Fabian made a sweeping motion towards the barbs, still embedded in the unconscious man's body, and they flew up to once again form a cocoon around their master. He began limping towards Surazal, who had made quick work of his remaining opponents. The cat-eyed man grinned as he wiped crimson blood off his sword with the rune-embroidered edge of his tunic. He regarded Fabian's dishevelled appearance, a stark contrast to his own unmarked body, and reached into the pocket of his breeches, retrieving a flower with lightly crushed petals and offering it to Fabian, who took it and gratefully pressed it to the wound on his chest. The red stain on his tunic gradually began to fade, and he sighed with obvious relief. Elijah recognised the bloom, having seen it so often among the numberless collection of things in Eldest's quarters as well as once seeing it blooming near his own house. Bloodlace.

Fabian was just about to press the now shrivelled flower to his infected arm, when Surazal pushed him down onto the ground with a cry. Elijah gasped as the air was forced out of Fabian's lungs upon impact.

Fabian looked at Surazal, who had landed on the grass next to him, in askance. But his visage paled as he took in what he saw.

A dagger had embedded itself in the side of Surazal's chest. Elijah could see its silver hilt from the distance. It looked . . . familiar, somehow. The feeling of recognition hung on the tip of his tongue like a forgotten word, but Elijah couldn't place where he recognised it from. Emotions rippled across Fabian's face, and he looked up to find out who had thrown the dagger. But he saw no one. Steeling his nerves, Fabian gripped the hilt of the dagger, pulling it out of Surazal. The Elder cried out in pain, his face scrunched up and pale as the blood rushed to the open wound in his side, and spilled onto the grass in a torrent of silver.

Wait, Elijah thought, *silver?*

He looked closer to ensure that his mind wasn't playing tricks on him. But it wasn't just his imagination. Surazal was bleeding silver.

"Something's wrong," Sebastian wheezed, as if his breath had been knocked out of him. He clutched at his breast, as if it was his heart that laboured, pumping what looked like liquid silver.

"Something is terribly, horribly wrong."

CHAPTER 22

IN HIS TEN years of being an Invisitus, Fabian thought he had seen it all.

He knew that Invisitae could heal themselves using bloodlace, that the flower would shrivel up and die after its capacity had been met.

He knew that Invisitae were a rare and strange species, that the mysterious powers they possessed were as beautiful as they were foreign.

He knew that Invisitae were far from human. That no human could jump as high, move as fast, fight as effortlessly.

But he also knew that no matter how different Invisitae were from humans, they both bled unvaryingly red.

Which would explain his confusion at the silver blood staining his tunic as it poured from the wound in his comrade's side.

Surazal's face was deathly pale, and his eyelids fluttering as he swam in and out of consciousness. Fabian pressed his hand to the wound in his side, and Surazal let out an animal growl, spit pooling near his mouth. The blood under his fingers seemed cold as ice, Fabian could feel it seep through his fingers.

It didn't feel like blood. Blood was warm and sticky, it oozed freely once freed, but lost the thrum of life within it once it left the body. But the liquid under his fingers felt frosty and alive, dribbling out slowly, but feeling every bit as alive as Fabian was.

It was almost as if a part of Surazal's body was leaching out of him.

As if the very essence of him was being leached away.

Fabian's mind raced. There had been rumours, there had been rumours of this happening, but he had never believed it. He didn't think it was possible. It couldn't be.

Fabian knew that the Change was irreversible, that once you became an Invisitus there was no going back. Or was there?

He looked at the dagger that lay forgotten next to his own sword, and fear dragged its frigid finger along his spine, sending ripples of ice through his veins. The dagger was identical to the one he possessed, the one that had been dipped in tainted water. The one that had made him who he was – that had made him *what* he was. But that was impossible – there was only one other dagger like it.

Two of a kind, just like him and Eric.

Footsteps approached him, but he dared not turn.

Two of a kind, of which one was lost forever. He knew it.
"Hello, *brother*."
Fabian ceased breathing.
Evidently he knew far less than he ought to.

CHAPTER 23

"STEP AWAY FROM the body, Fabian."

Fabian recognised the voice. How could he not? It had haunted his dreams for the last ten years. But still, there was something inherently wrong with it. Something innately . . . *other*.

"Have all these years made you impudent, brother? I said *step away from the man*," the voice snarled, and Fabian cringed unwillingly. Surazal was deathly still beside him, a corpse in the making.

"No," he said, his voice hoarse with a decade's worth of emotion. There was so much he wanted to say, but he couldn't form the words around the odd mixture of love and abhorrence in his throat.

"No?" Eric laughed humourlessly. His laugh made it all the more obvious that there was something unnatural about him. "You abandon me for ten years and that's the first thing you'll say to me?"

Guilt and shame flooded him.

"I thought you were *dead*," Fabian choked out.

This warranted another bark of laughter.

"How could you be certain if you didn't bother to check?"

Fabian gulped and hung his head in the pretence of looking at Surazal, mumbling something unintelligible.

Eric gave an impatient snort.

"If you refuse to admit your mistake—"

"I didn't make a mistake. You were gone," Fabian said.

"What did you say?" Eric said.

"I *did* check. Your heart wasn't beating," he repeated, loudly.

"If you're going to lie to me, the least you can do is say it *to my face!*" While speaking, Eric strode over to Fabian, gripped his shoulder, and turned him to face him.

Fabian gave a cry of surprise and recoiled. The man in front of him was indisputably his brother, but there was more to him somehow. Both brothers had been blessed with an aquiline nose and fine, high cheekbones, but Fabian's seemed elegant while Eric's were harrowing. His skin held an unhealthy pallor, as if he was ailing, but the crushing strength of his grip on Fabian's shoulder said otherwise. His skin was mapped by a tracery of veins so blue they were almost black, a sharp contrast against the papery white of his skin. Eric's lips were like a bloodstain on the milky skin of his face, accentuated by the unforgiving slope of his nose. Green eyes coloured with malice stared unflinching into Fabian's, and Fabian realised with a start that there were identical gold designs on both of Eric's irises.

"What are you?" Fabian said, pity colouring his words.

"Now, now, you've had your fun." Fabian winced as another familiar voice joined the fray.

"Zachariah," Fabian choked out. The hand at his collar was making it hard to speak.

"You heard me, let him go," Zachariah said by way of reply.

Eric bared his teeth in disgust and dragged Fabian to his feet before letting go of his collar and standing behind Zachariah. Fabian massaged his neck. He looked around for the silver dagger, but couldn't find it anywhere. He narrowed his eyes in confusion, but dismissed the thought to the back of his mind.

"Reversing the Change? I should've known you were behind this," Fabian said, eyes betraying nothing. He stood in front of Surazal, as if to shield his body.

Zachariah smirked.

"Oh, this was hardly my idea. This was entirely your brother's." Fabian's eyes widened fractionally, but he masked it with a cold indifference. "He's such a brilliant man, wouldn't you say? I should thank you for leaving him behind, he's been such a valuable addition to our family."

Fabian flinched at the word family, his lack of one being made more and more acute.

"How?"

Zachariah motioned for Eric to explain.

"It was simple, really. Invisitae are such feeble creatures. You have a laughable weakness for steel. It makes you lose your affinity, makes your lose your ability to teleport, makes you human. I reckoned there must be some composition of steel that severs this connection completely. I was right. That, dipped in tainted water, is the perfect cure for your disease."

He spat the last word at Fabian, who flinched slightly, despite himself.

"Except I haven't managed to create the water once again . . ." Eric said.

Fabian remained impassive. Zachariah had moved closer to him, closer to Surazal.

"Brilliant, isn't it?"

"Ingenious," Fabian said coolly, masking the fact that he did, in fact, think it was brilliant. "Why did you do it, Eric?"

Eric fought to school his features, to mask his true feelings, but in the end he gave in.

"You know not the things I have seen, how much I have suffered. Yes, I had died. My heart had ceased to beat. But he saved me. He brought me back."

Fabian remembered the inhuman anger reflected in his eyes, remembered the intricate gold symbol in his irises. His heart leapt.

"What are you?" he whispered, accusingly. "What have they made you?"

With a feral sneer, Eric replied, "I am *Umbra*. I am stronger than you will ever be."

Fabian shuddered involuntarily. He could see it now, the glint of bone under flesh, the sickly sweet scent of decay on his brother's lips. He truly was *umbra*, a mere echo of his former self.

"Who did this to you? Whose shadow are you?"

Eric cocked his head to one side, a gesture so inhuman it sent shivers up his spine.

You and I both know the answer, Zachariah's voice tickled his momentarily vulnerable mind.

Fabian's cracked lips parted as the name was wrenched from his mouth:

"Lazarus."

Zachariah glowed with the elation of having permeated Fabian's mind.

"Now step away from Surazal. He's not yours to save," Zachariah said, stepping closer.

" He is a brother to me," Fabian growled through his teeth.

"What does that make me then, *brother*?" Eric screamed and charged at Fabian, years of festered hurt and anger contorting his face.

Fabian hesitated, and Eric's fist careened into his face. Fabian was taken aback by his brother's strength. His knuckles were as strong as iron. They had fought before, when they were teenagers, but that had been fun and games.

Fabian spat out a mouthful of blood, and looked up at his brother, searching his features for a sign of him, the *true* Eric. But all he could see was a puppet.

Eric lunged at him once again, and Fabian reached out to the metal barbs that lay scattered around Surazal. They responded immediately and levitated in front of his person, forcing Eric to step back.

"This is not who you are, Eric! Try to remember!" Fabian's heart leapt around in his chest frantically.

"Why should I remember when it was *you* who forgot me?" Eric sneered, and lunged again.

Fabian winced in pain for Eric as his shoulder connected with a few barbs, but the Umbra didn't seem to register the pain.

"I never, ever forgot you," Fabian said, keeping his eyes trained on Eric as he circled him in search for an opening.

"Liar!" Eric bellowed. He ducked below Fabian's barbs and hit him square in the chest, sending the younger man sprawling to the ground. Before he hit the ground, he thought of a grassy patch a few feet away, near an overturned cart, and teleported there.

He landed with an "oomph!" on the ground, his head hitting wood. He heard a gasp emanate from behind the cart, and his eyes met the frightened, blue ones of Elijah.

The boy's eyes grew wider, and Elijah clamped a hand over his own mouth. Fabian's blood ran cold.

What is he doing here? What if they find him? he thought, remembering his promise to the boy's mother. Then, ashamed, he thought, *Just how much did he see?*

He raised his fingers to his lips in warning, and turned back to face his brother who stood screaming,

"Come back and face me like a man, you coward!"

Fabian teleported to his brother's side, and jabbed him in his side with his elbow. By the time Eric had turned around, he had teleported once again and done the same to his other side.

"I can never forget about you," Fabian said and punctuated each word by teleporting away from Eric's wrath and landing another blow, wearing him out.

Eric stood, confused and heaving, and Fabian decided to try one last time.

"How could I, Eric?" he said, sadly. "We're brothers."

The anger drained out of Eric's face as he was transported back to another time, when Fabian had said these exact same words. A time before all the pain and the hatred, a time when it was just them. Two of a kind.

Fabian watched the myriad of emotions flit across his brother's face, hoping, praying, *pleading* that he had managed to get through. Then, suddenly, Eric shot out an arm and grabbed Fabian by the collar.

Fabian closed his eyes. He had failed.

He felt his body being wrenched forward and crushed. No, not crushed. *Embraced.*

Fabian opened his eyes in shock. He felt a wetness on his shoulder, where Eric rested his head. *Was he crying?*

Fabian raised a hand to his own face, and found tears spilling from his numb eyes and coursing down his cheeks. *Why am I crying?*

He curled his arms around his brother's back, returning the embrace.

A few moments passed, and he felt Eric withdraw hastily.

"Don't say a word," Eric said. His voice was thick with tears, but he sounded more like himself.

The brothers wiped furiously at their cheeks, embarrassed at expressing emotion, even when there was nobody to see it.

That's strange, Fabian thought. He looked around, and was met with empty landscape. He stepped backward. He saw nothing but grassland for miles, with the exception of the cart and the village beyond it.

Where were Zachariah and Surazal?

"Brother, where are the others?" Fabian asked, and Eric looked around too. Confusion flitted across his face, chased away by guilty shame. He wouldn't meet Fabian's eye.

"What are you hiding, Eric? Tell me." Fabian's voice could have cut glass.

"This was part of the plan," he said. "Lazarus wanted me to distract you, so that we could rescue Surazal."

"Bring Surazal back?" Fabian's head was pounding. "How did he know Surazal would be here?"

Eric looked away.

Fabian felt sick.

"Do you mean Surazal . . . it can't be."

Eric looked up and nodded, slowly.

"*Surazal was the informant?*" Fabian's normal baritone hitched up an octave.

Eric opened his mouth, as if to say more, but he looked at a place above Fabian's right shoulder and his eyes widened. Fabian heard a sinister laugh near his right ear, followed by the words,

"You weren't supposed to hear that."

Fabian attempted to whirl around, but someone pressed a blade to his throat. It nicked the skin under his chin, and hot blood spilled from his skin.

"Surazal," he choked out. The wielder of the knife to his neck chortled.

"That's right. Me." Fabian heard the clinking of chains, and felt Surazal bind his hands behind him with the chains. Of course, they were steel.

Surazal proceeded to tie his legs, and stepped back to survey his work. Surazal smirked at Fabian's expression of betrayal, and Fabian hawked a gob of spit at the man's feet.

"How are you even alive?" Fabian asked, "That cut had nearly killed you."

"Zachariah may not have the illusory prowess of that little girl, but he most certainly doesn't disappoint."

It all started to make sense. How the dagger seemed to materialise from nowhere, how strange Surazal's wound had been, the disappearance of the dagger. Everything.

As Fabian watched, Zachariah materialised in front of him. He bowed.

"Your words delight me, Master."

Fabian's eyes bugged.

"Master? But aren't you Lazarus's right hand man?" Surazal's smile widened as he took in Fabian's confusion. "The only man you'd answer to is . . ."

Fabian's shoulders tensed. His eyes took on a wild look.

"Surazal," he said, his voice small. "It's a palindrome for Lazarus. How could I have missed it?"

Surazal clasped his hands in mock pride.

"At last, I have played all my cards. Such a shame that you had none from the start."

Fabian begged to differ, but his trump was not a very reliable one. He had only managed it once, and he was unsure of whether or not he could muster up the strength to do it again.

"Why did you do it?" Fabian said, biding his time.

Lazarus looked at him fondly, his cat eyes gleaming.

"Such an honourable man you are, yet so naïve, believing that everyone needs a reason for doing something."

He came closer to Fabian.

"Perhaps my only reason was that I *could*. Just like I can do this." With that, he smiled insincerely and vanished, reappearing with his sword drawn behind Eric.

Fabian opened his mouth to scream a warning, to save his brother, but he couldn't make a sound. He saw Zachariah smile and waggle a finger at him teasingly, concentrating on blocking the passage of sound. The silence felt like a slap coupled with the strain of his vocal chords.

Eric looked at Fabian bewildered, and smiled sheepishly, like he would when he'd made Fabian bear the blame for something he'd done, when they were children. Then Surazal's sword descended, and Eric's smile was cleaved in half.

CHAPTER 24

ELIJAH SQUEEZED HIS eyes shut.

He hoped it would shut out the sights he had just seen, but the image was etched into his mind like the runes on Surazal's clothes.

Surazal. His own mentor was the leader of the Occidierum. A warrior being trained by his worst enemy – how fitting.

Everything began piecing itself together: the catlike flash of his eyes, how the Bellator's identity was revealed, how Surazal roped himself into being sent to save her. It all made sense, even to him.

He glanced at his comrades. Jarrod's face was turned away, and he was shaking with silent sobs. Sebastian, on the other hand, glowered at Surazal. His body hummed with rage, and Elijah felt badly for him. It was not easy seeing the person you admired in their true colours, especially if they were coloured crimson from head to toe.

Elijah himself shook with silent grief. Fabian had been reunited with his long lost brother, only to lose him once again. The image of his silent scream was a scar that wouldn't soon leave Elijah's thoughts.

"Why shed tears over carrion, Fabian? I returned him to his natural state. You should be *thanking* me."

Elijah felt something inside him snap. A tidal wave of anger swept through his being, and he felt the winds caress his fingertips, goading him to do the very thing he was itching to do.

But Sebastian beat him to it. The older boy sprang out from his hiding place and screamed,

"You bastard!"

Elijah quelled the winds momentarily and watched breathlessly as, for the first time, Sebastian ran towards his idol with nothing but hatred in his eyes.

*

Sebastian may not have been a fighter by affinity, but he was a fighter by nature and that was all that mattered.

While charging at Lazarus, he realised belatedly that this was the first time the older man had really *looked* at him. His eyes widened at first, shocked by his unexpected appearance, but then they grew disinterested and he waved at Zachariah absently, instructing him to deal with the boy.

Sebastian cleared his mind and imagined himself stepping into Surazal's skin. The first time he had morphed, he had slipped into the new visage effortlessly, albeit he had no idea he was doing so. And with every time he had consciously morphed since, he came closer and closer to attaining that first unconscious effortlessness.

To defeat your enemy, you must know his weaknesses. Surazal had taught him that. He would use his own advice against Surazal's own lackey, a person so devoted that he would most certainly be reluctant to hurt his "master".

He had always been an eager student, and even after everything, he was still eager to prove to Surazal that he *was* worth noticing.

*

The moment he saw Surazal turn away from Sebastian, Elijah knew he wouldn't sit still. The sea was strong and its winds were stronger still, but Elijah was the Stormbringer and strong winds were the best kind, as far as he was concerned.

He felt his eyes silver over, and he felt his senses sharpen, as if his mind was filtering out any distractions. He could taste the salty tang of the sea, and smell the distinct scent of steel and brine. He could sense the vast amounts of moisture within the air, and he had an idea.

He created a cocoon of air to shield himself from the others' gaze, and made it rise into the air, taking him with it. Simultaneously, he began gathering droplets of water from the moisture-rich air, and added them to the cocoon he had created.

He rose higher and higher into the hair, giddy with the sudden loss of oxygen and the rush that using his power gave him. The sky became darker as he rose, the atmosphere becoming frigid enough for the water to condense and sheathe him in a huge, grey cloud.

Elijah felt the thrum of energy emanating from the cocoon he had created, the arsenal of power he had accumulated in one place sparking off one another.

He sent a gale of wind to move Lazarus away from Sebastian, who was engaged in fearsome battle with Zachariah, and Fabian, who stood motionless. He fancied he could hear Lazarus yelp as he was buffeted away by his wind.

Then, taking care to create protective cocoons around Jarrod, Fabian and Sebastian, Elijah let loose the droplets of water in a fearsome, hammering bout of rain, concentrating the brunt of it on the two dreadful men.

Elijah's rush of victory was short-lived. He'd hoped his gales of wind and the torrential downpour would deter the two men, but they seemed to do little to deter them. He needed more than just a distraction, he needed a spark to completely rivet their attention.

A spark.

Elijah swallowed, hesitating momentarily. What he was about to attempt was incredible, completely unbelievable. *I've never managed to control it consciously before*, he thought, *I doubt I can, even now*. But before now, Elijah had never had reason to control the lightning he created.

"There's no use being afraid of it, Elijah. You control the power," he whispered to himself as Adara had, in his first lesson with Elder Lucian. He smiled, invigorated with a sense of urgency and newfound confidence. He could do it. He simply knew it.

Elijah willed himself to feel the surge of power through his veins, and concentrated the power into his fingertips. Elijah's palms became hypersensitive, and he felt pinpricks of electricity in the pads of his fingers. To test the waters, Elijah snapped his fingers, trying – for the first time ever – to willingly summon a bolt of lightning. He'd expected he'd have to try a few times before he succeeded, but he was pleasantly surprised when sparks began dancing over his fingers, warming them. Aiming for a patch of grass next to Lazarus, he folded his palm into a fist, and opened it seconds later. A blue flash of light streaked from his open palms and hit the grass, creating a muddy crater where Lazarus had just been standing.

He saw the man squint up at Elijah, and Elijah created another flash of lightning that lit the cloud he was in, the silhouette of his body showing up dramatically. He saw apprehension flicker across the man's face and, having fulfilled his goal of making an impactful entrance, he began his descent.

Elijah smiled. He was the Stormbringer. And a storm he would bring.

*

Jarrod had never thought much about hell, but he was certain that it would look something like the scene playing out in front of him.

To his right, Sebastian and Zachariah were sparring. Zachariah had a confused and slightly frightened look on his face, as If he was worried that Sebastian would tell him off. But that was rather understandable considering Sebastian wore the face of the man he revered. Jarrod never thought he would get to see a fight between two men who thought Surazal hung the moon – even though for different reasons – and he wanted nothing more than for it to be over.

Jarrod hated the idea of fighting. Surazal's classes had been his own personal hell until Elijah had come along. But he had to admit, the fight between Sebastian and Zachariah was a wondrous experience. They parried and swiped as if they were birds in flight.

Jarrod watched as Zachariah slashed at Sebastian's sword arm and the boy cried out in pain, blood streaming down and mixing with the rain-soaked grass. Zachariah screamed victoriously, but his victory was short-lived as

Elijah sent an arc of lightning towards him. The bolt hit him square in the chest, and the man flew towards the edge of the cliff before precariously skidding to a halt at the edge. The man's shirtfront smoked, and Jarrod could make out the charred red of his flesh even through the blinding rain surrounding him.

Jarrod swivelled his head to regard Elijah, and was once again taken aback by how much he had changed. In just a few weeks, Elijah had cultivated a body and demeanour that matched his awe-inspiring power. Jarrod could smell the ozone around his friend; he could feel the aftershocks of the gusts of wind he sent towards Lazarus, feel his hair rising with the electricity coursing through his body as the lightning bolts charged the air around him. The rain, which fell in sheets, avoided him – though Jarrod suspected that was Elijah's own doing.

But the thing that really caught his attention was the absolute quiet that surrounded Fabian. The ropes of rain, the flashes of lightning, the sounds of swords clanging; it all seemed to bounce off Fabian, as if he had created a barrier between himself and the world. As if he had withdrawn into himself so much that there was little chance of him coming back.

*

When Fabian saw Eric fall, he felt numb. His jaw went slack, his vocal chords stopped straining. He forgot how to stand, and sank to his knees. He heard nothing, felt nothing but utter numbness. He looked at what was left of his brother, and watched in silence as his body turned to ash and blew away with the wind. A hollow ache spread from his chest to the rest of his body, as if his blood too was vaporising.

Then Lazarus opened his mouth, and Fabian *felt*.

He felt it start in his chest, a sizzle, like hot wax had been dripped on his chest. He felt it spread, then, from his chest to his arms to his legs to his head and he felt every part of become energised, as if the energy his brother had possessed filled the empty spaces within him. Fabian shut his eyes, and focused on the particles of the chains binding him.

You have a laughable vulnerability to steel, he heard Eric say, *Invisitae are so feeble*.

He was right. After all, what was steel but a combination of metals?

He awakened his consciousness, and used it to probe the metals in the chain binding him. They were reluctant to obey him, at first, but he coaxed them awake. He imagined he was a kettle, and once he had the attention of every single molecule of metal within the chain, he imagined him pouring his energy into them.

Immediately, he felt the metal grow hotter on his skin. He could feel the power leaving him in waves, soaking into the metal of the chain and leaving behind a cold, empty feeling, a feeling of loss, like losing Eric once again.

He missed that energy. He missed Eric.

Eric. The scars from ten years ago cut afresh once again. Death of the brother to be borne again.

Tears scalded his cheeks, metal scalded his skin but his heart remained as frigid as the rain pooling around his feet.

He had to let go, it was the only way.

He let the metals out of their molecular prison and he let his anger, fear and sorrow out with them in a deafening wail.

CHAPTER 25

ELIJAH'S BODY FELT ripe with power. He could feel the electricity he wielded like a lance course through his body. It warmed him from the inside. Controlling the winds hadn't made him feel nearly this invulnerable. He landed before Lazarus, who had recovered his poise in the few seconds since he first saw Elijah.

"Impressive show of lights, boy, but I do consider myself a failure of a teacher, considering your absolute refusal to touch a blade," Lazarus said, pointedly staring at his full scabbard while twirling his own sword absentmindedly.

"You are no teacher, you are nothing but a filthy traitor!" Elijah hissed, sending another bolt of lightning his way, only to be deflected by the flat of Lazarus's blade.

"I didn't want this any more than you did, and I *refuse* to be stuck as an Invisitus – as a monster – for the rest of my life. So watch your tongue, boy, or I'll have to cut it out of you," he said, lunging at Elijah once again.

Elijah made an elaborate upward motion with his hands, and the headwind made Lazarus skid backwards, leaving lumps of muddy grass dragged up by his heels.

"I'd like to see you try," Elijah said. Lazarus sneered and assumed his stance once again, ready to lunge.

A terrible keening sound filled the air, cutting through the rain and sound of boots squelching with an edge as sharp as a knife. The suddenness of the sound resulted in an abrupt stop to the rain, as Elijah relinquished control of the elements in his surprise. The sound seemed all-pervading, as if the very Earth was howling in sorrow.

Elijah looked around, bewildered, until his eyes found Fabian. The terrible wail came from his lips. The shackles on the man's wrists and ankles were turning bright red, rippling as if they were melting from the heat that was emanating from Fabian. Elijah saw sweat and rain rise off him in puffs of steam as the metal sizzled and hissed, a chorus to the lament.

"This is impossible . . ." Lazarus said, his eyes nearly double their size. "No Invisitus can escape steel."

Elijah covered his ears as Fabian's cry swelled to a crescendo, and stopped abruptly. The silence was deafening, pregnant with the promise of something unexpected.

Fabian opened his eyes, and the chains shattered.

Before the now-molten metal could hit the ground, Fabian swooped them together and sent them careening towards Lazarus,who turned on his heel and vanished seconds before the metal made contact with him.

Fabian sank to his knees and Elijah ran to stop him from pitching forward into the grass, the storminess of the sky dissipating.

"Jarrod!" Elijah screamed, supporting Fabian's full weight until Sebastian reached the two.

Jarrod regained control of his limbs and ran towards Fabian, slipping on the slick grass.

He regarded Fabian's wounds with clinical precision. There were terrible burns on his wrists and ankles, and the infected wound on his arm needed cleaning before he could heal it. There were chances that there was still metal embedded in the wound, and Jarrod couldn't close the wound without checking.

"I'll need supplies. I can't heal him without them." Jarrod stumbled over the words.

Fabian's eyes opened at that.

"Take me to Marian," he whispered hoarsely.

Elijah nodded, understanding. "Jarrod, Sebastian. You have to take him to the farm. My mother can help you."

"What will you do without our help?" Sebastian asked. Jarrod looked away from Fabian towards Elijah. Right at this moment, he looked like a scared child. Nothing like the Stormbringerhe was just moments ago. But Elijah set his jaw, and swiped his brown hair off his forehead. A determined look had etched itself into his features, his eyes windows into a warrior's soul.

"I have to save Adara. Only I can do it," he said, squaring his shoulders and looking at the cliff opposite the monstrous metal building. Like this, it wasn't difficult imagining him as the Stormbringer, the Sky's warrior.

"Besides," he smiled kindly, once again a young boy, "You've always wanted to see a farm, haven't you?"

Jarrod smiled, despite everything, and nodded.

Elijah helped the two boys balance Fabian between them.

"Tell Mother I'm safe," he said.

Jarrod stifled a laugh at the irony, and said instead,

"Tell her yourself, when you get back."

Sebastian looked at Elijah with a mixture of awe and worry.

"Be safe," he said.

Fabian met Elijah's eyes with his own and beckoned for him to come closer. Fabian reached out a hand to brush Elijah's hair out of his eyes. His voice, when he spoke, was raspy, but swelled with pride.

"The dagger chose well. Light the sky, Stormbringer."

*

Marian was busying herself making tea in the kitchen when a sound like the roof had just caved in came from the barn.

She rushed out, frying pan in hand – an accessory she now rarely left the kitchen without.

She walked over to the barn, and when she saw the state of the barn roof, muttered a string of obscenities that could make a sailor blush.

Putting on a face braver than she felt inside, she kicked open the barn door. Inside, stood two boys, supporting a handsome but worn-out young man between them. The man smiled, gritting his teeth with pain, as Marion stepped closer, palm covering her mouth when she saw who it was.

Quickly recovering composure, she quirked her features into a frown – a look, she thought, more appropriate.

"Why is it," she said, brandishing the pan, "that you always show up here with an intention to kill, or an intention to die?"

The boys on either side of him paled, but Fabian's skin took on a healthier glow. He laughed softly, and Marion blushed, pleased.

"It gives me an excuse to see you, doesn't it?"

CHAPTER 26

EVER SINCE SHE had been taken in by the Invisitae at the tender age of two, Adara had been taught that grogginess was as deadly as a blade poised at her throat. A sentient mind could be the difference between life and death, she'd been told by Sapiens so often that she could remember it better than she could her parents' faces. But despite her best efforts, Adara couldn't shake the bleariness she felt when she finally awoke after being injected with the liquefied steel.

It must have been just a few hours, a day at most, since she'd been abducted from the Brotherhood's labyrinth. But to Adara, it felt like she'd emerged from the ordeal as a sixty-year-old woman. Her head throbbed, and her tongue felt like sandpaper in her equally parched mouth. The frigidness of the floor seeped through her ragged pants and froze her joints, making them ache and creak as she tried to shift her position on the uncomfortable ground. A similar cold seeped into her wrists, which were bound together by a slim circlet of some kind. *Steel*, she thought, simultaneously praying that she was wrong. It was highly unlikely, however. Luck had not been on her side, of late.

What finally shook her out of her daze was the rumble of her stomach. She felt it emanate from deep within her abdomen, and rumble all the way down to her toes. Was it her imagination, or did the sound seem to carry? Adara tried opening her eyes, but they felt glued shut. Instead, she let her consciousness probe around her, to give her a better grasp of her surroundings.

Opening her mind up to her surroundings made Adara acutely aware of the subtle shifts around her, and she was taken aback by the extreme lack of any. The very air around her felt stale and dry, as if it had been locked inside the space forever. Extremely unlike the vision she'd transmitted to Fabian, she realised, praying that she hadn't been wrong in her ideas of her general location.

Adara blindly groped the area with her mind, and recoiled with an agonised cry as she reached an unexpected barrier at a distance of approximately five feet in front of her. She tried once again, exploring a radius of five feet around her, but she couldn't get past the impenetrable barrier. Her heartbeat sped up and she swallowed, her parched throat scratching audibly in the stillness. She threw her consciousness towards the ceiling in a growing frenzy, and flinched as she encountered the same resistance. There was only one material her powers couldn't get past, and that was . . .

"Steel," she said, her normally melodious voice sounding gruff and deep with disuse. "They've thrown me into a steel trap." Her eyes fluttered open in abject terror.

Adara calmed her frenzied breathing and tried searching for cracks and apertures within the room, but was left vastly disappointed. If she had been put into the room, surely there was some way to get out of it. Swinging her bound hands to give her momentum, she sat up, her back glacial from the contact with the steel wall. Suddenly, she heard the sound of laboured footsteps coming from outside the steel entrapment, and Adara hastily pretended to be unconscious once again, keeping her consciousness sharp and focused to be able to read the person's identity. The beat of the footsteps were irregular, as if the person was limping. The sound gave her hope; if the person was weak, she might be able to overpower them and get out of her cell. Perhaps then, she could find help.

Adara heard the sound of metal grinding against metal, and sensed a narrow steel shutter rising off the ground, and heard a person of considerable size hobble into the enclosure. Adara probed at the person's mind with her own, but encountered an impenetrable resistance. Whoever had placed the wards in the person's mind knew what they were doing. Immediately, she threw up walls of her own, shocked at her lack of forethought.

A low chuckle escaped from the person's mouth, confirming that the person was a man. Adara's eyelids twitched; she recognised that mirthless laugh, but couldn't place it.

"You may be an exceptional illusionist, Adara," the man said in a measured baritone, "but you've always been a lousy actress."

Adara's heart stopped, and she couldn't help stop her hands from trembling. She opened her eyes coolly, and stared into the grey eyes she loathed so completely.

"Zachariah," she spat his name out, as if expelling a foul taste. "You look well."

He most certainly didn't. He looked as if he'd run headfirst into a horse-drawn carriage. He leaned heavily on his left leg, and he winced with every step he took. He had a thick bandage wrapped round his chest, which was splotched with dark stains.

He smiled grimly at the jab, but offered nothing in return. He opened his arms in a mockery of an embrace, and stepped closer to her, towering over her crouched form. He did this only to intimidate her, but she wouldn't let it get to her. She turned her gaze sharply away from him, focusing instead on a speck of dust on the floor between his legs

"The steel should have worn out of your system by now, no need to look so pathetic." He laughed, and she snarled at him menacingly.

Before she could register it, his hand shot out to grab her chin, and jerk it up to his own. He scrutinised her features coldly, and she took savage pleasure in noting the bruises and cuts peppering his skin. She struggled against him, but there was little she could do with her hands bound behind her back.

"Don't you dare, you mangy mutt!" he snarled. Adara smirked, and spat at his face. A glob of her spit landed perfectly in his eye, and he sputtered and flinched back with disgust.

He pawed at the spittle on his face, and Adara sneered as his face purpled with indignation. Before she knew what was happening, he struck her across the face with the back of her hand.

The blow sent Adara reeling, and her head banged against the wall. The sound of skinand bone against metal reverberated in her buzzing ears, and she felt the blood rush to her tender cheek. The pounding in her skull returned once again, but she ignored it, and turned to face Zachariah again, gazing steadfastly into his squinted eyes.

Adara smiled, the tender flesh of her cheek stinging with the action, though her smile appeared more suited to a grimace.

"Poor Zachariah. Still stinging from Sapiens's unwillingness to trust you, is it? He's evidently moved on, but I see you haven't,"she said.

A growl grew in Zachariah's throat, and he retorted,

"Sapiens is the biggest fool I have ever encountered. I am much better off with Lazarus as my master."

Adara snorted derisively, which elicited another slap from Zachariah. He struck her hard enough to split the tender skin of her lip, and she cringed at the tinny smell of her own blood.

"Get used to the smell, girl. That's just a taste of what'll happen to you if you don't cooperate with us," he said, noticing her wince.

Adara spat blood to the side, the contrast of the deep crimson against the shiny metal was startling.

"What do you want from me?" she rasped.

Zachariah barked a laugh and said,

"That's not for me to say. Stand up."

Adara refused to move, the fight rising up in her throat. Zachariah's eyes darkened with rage. He grabbed a fistful of her matted curls and yanked hard, Adara biting her cheek to stop herself from yowling.

"I said," he punctuated his words by pulling her upright and bringing his face inches from her own: "Stand. Up."

Adara braced herself for another blow, but it didn't come. The man shifted his grip to her elbow and propelled her in front of him, jabbing her in the small of her back to keep her from stopping. He pushed her through the opening in the steel room, all the while keeping a strong grip on her elbow. They went through a short passage. He marched her past a mirror, and she couldn't help but steal a glance at her reflection.

Her skin was pale and sallow, the hollows beneath her violet eyes blue-black with exhaustion. Her hair framed her face like a mane, standing out in matted clumps. But what grabbed her attention was the thin rope of steel circling her slender wrists. The circlet was thin and pliant, but it held her wrists in place. If only she could figure out a way to slice the slender fastening apart . . .

Before she could search for an object sharp enough to break her shackles, Zachariah bound a coarse cloth around her eyes and Adara was plunged into darkness.

"You'll get what you deserve soon enough, ingrate," he spat at her, but she said nothing. He grabbed her arm forcefully and dragged her onwards, Adara stumbling as she tried to keep up with his swift hobble. She heard a door open and the tang of briny wind reached her, helping clear the haze in her head. They stepped through the doorway, and Adara had scarcely heard the distant crash of waves on a rocky shore before they teleported.

*

Elijah watched wistfully as the trio hobbled away from him with their backs turned, and his eyes remained trained on their position long after they'd teleported away, and the plumes of dust in their wake had settled. How badly he'd wanted to return to the farm, his home, and see his mother again! His heart twisted with a pang of longing so potent, he could hardly bear it. But he knew now, more than anyone, the danger Adara– and by proxy, all of the Invisitae – were in. He was the Stormbringer, in charge of protecting his people, especially the prophesised Protector, the Bellator.

He drew his eyes away from the grass and surveyed the wide expanse of land in front of him. Gently grassy hillocks rolled endlessly to his left, washed green and fresh with the rain he'd called down. To his right, he could hear the rhythmic roar of the waves as they broke against the resolute crags of rock on the side of the cliff. A few miles ahead, he could see the monstrosity of the metal building disfiguring the pleasing green atmosphere like gangrene. Elijah's lips curled in distaste at the acrid taste of metal mingling with the sharp tang of salt in the mild wind.

How far he'd come, in just a few short months. He'd left behind the comfort of a barren home, and been thrown headfirst into danger that took him to breathtakingly luscious regions. He barked a humourless laugh at the irony of his situation.

He squinted his eyes as he looked into the sky. It had returned to an astounding shade of periwinkle, with a few cottony clouds meandering across the heavens. This looked nothing like the virulent skies he'd seen in his dream. Perhaps he was over-thinking the significance of his dream. He could control the elements to bring forth fantastic storms, but even he was not a seer. Perhaps it was nothing. But he couldn't deny the fact that he had only found himself in Castlemartin because of that very dream.

Elijah shook his head and steadied his shoulders, getting ready to summon a concealing mist to hide his approach towards the steel monstrosity, when he heard the air behind him split, followed by a smattering of soft thuds, the sound of footsteps in the mud. He whirled around, using the adrenaline coursing through his veins to help summon himself some lightning, and gave a silent prayer of thanks that he'd finally mastered his control over the unexpected portent.

Elijah faced a group of approximately ten men, outfitted in identical black gear with spidery runes etched into the fabric. The very armour he'd seen sported by Surazal-Lazarus – and Fabian. He lowered his arms, recalling the lightning. The oldest warrior amongst the group turned to face Elijah. He wore a face Elijah recognised very well, from the hours he'd spent with him. But Elijah had never seen that face contorted with the fury and concern it currently wore.

"How could you be so foolish?" Sapiens spat at Elijah. All traces of the kindly old man had vanished. In his space stood a seasoned warrior, whose age had in no way dulled the fire in his veins. Elijah stepped back, intimidated.

Sapiens stalked towards Elijah, closely followed by Lucian, wearing a similar mask of exasperation and concern.

"You could've *died*. What would we have done then?" Sapiens said.

Elijah grew indignant.

"I'm the Stormbringer. I can handle myself."

"You are a *child*," Lucian said. Despite the concern dripping from his words, the truth stung Elijah.

"But I have to save her! It's my duty—"

"It is *my* duty, as the Eldest of the Brotherhood, to protect both of you. You may be the Stormbringer, Elijah, but you are still a fledgling. It's a wonder you managed to travel here without losing a limb. Or worse." All the anger drained away from Sapien's face, and concern rushed in to take its place. He placed an arm on the shoulders of the dejected Elijah, saying, "I can't let this continue. My men and I can handle the Occidierum and bring Adara back. You have to return to the Brotherhood."

"I can't simply give up now!" Elijah screamed, his desperationmounting. "Surazal has Adara, and who knows what he'll do to her." Sapiens's eyes widened and he stepped back in shock. The whole group of men looked aghast, as if they'd been struck by one of Elijah's lightning bolts.

"Surazal is one of the Occidierum?" Lucian echoed.

"Surazal *leads* the Occidierum," Elijah confirmed, drinking in the expressions of growing horror on their faces. "He is Lazarus."

Lucian turned to Sapiens, who remained immobile.

"This means he knows everything! Who Adara is, what she knows . . ."

"What she knows? What does that mean?"Elijah asked.

"Elijah, listen to me,"Sapiens responded urgently, "Do you remember what I had told you? About there being only two living people who know the Fountain's location?"

Elijah nodded. "You and your new apprentice."

Sapiens swallowed.

"The Bellator was too important, too volatile, too powerful to entrust to just one mentor. She is the only female Invisitus we know of, she has always been special. We couldn't afford for her to lose out on her training in case her mentor was harmed. And so, in addition to Fabian, I took her under my wing."

Realisation dawned on Elijah.

"Adara knows where the Fountain is. That's why they wanted her, and her alone."

Sapiens nodded, gravely.

"The identity of Lazarus changes everything. I had no idea that the Occidierum had infiltrated so deeply into our community. We might need your help after all," he said, and Elijah tried not to show his relief.

Sapiens's wide-set shoulders folded into themselves, making him appear old and tired.

"I have managed to do so little for you, Elijah. You still have such a long way to go. But I can do one more thing for you."

He disappeared and reappeared seconds later, holding a long, thin bundle wrapped in brown cloth, tied with string. He untied the string, and beckoned Elijah to unfold the cloth. Elijah did so, and his eyebrows rose almost to his hairline.

Resting on Sapiens's outstretched palms was the most beautiful sword Elijah had ever seen. The hilt was covered in spidery runes akin to the ones on Sapiens's own attire, and a jewel of the deepest blue was set within it. Elijah reached out to touch the hit, and found it was surprisingly warm to the touch, as if a crackling fire smouldered within the hilt. Elijah looked at Sapiens expectantly, and he motioned for the boy to take the sword. The hilt moulded itself into Elijah's grip, as if it was but an extension of his own arm. He touched the edge of the tempered metal of the blade, and shivered at its cool touch.

Elijah swung the sword through the air a few times, testing its weight and balance. His heart surged at the whoosh of the sword cleaving through the air. He met Sapiens's twinkling eyes with his own.

"The sword is called Tempest. It's been made especially for you by one of our most skilled smiths, from the best metals we have access to." He smiled. "It can weather the strongest of inundations, and can even withstand your lightning." Elijah grinned from ear to ear.

He unsheathed the sword Sebastian had given him, and placed Tempest in the scabbard. Immediately, he felt a longing to reach for the hilt, but instead he busied himself with rearranging his armour instead.

"Now that you're ready, we have an important battle ahead of us. I'm almost certain they will try to torture the information out of Adara, and we must not allow it to happen at all costs," Sapiens addressed his comrades.

"Do not forget that rescuing Adara is our number one priority. We can give Lazarus what he deserves after we have secured her. For without the Bellator, there is little hope for the Brotherhood.

"I cannot say for certain what the outcome of this battle will be, but I must say this: I have no doubt that we will all do our utmost to protect the Bellator. They say that fortune favours the brave, so we must seize that fortune today. We have no choice but to do so. *Vias nostras infinitam*, my brothers."

Elijah looked at the faces of the men around him. In this short while, he'd found himself an entire family. He would be honoured to fight alongside them. He tilted his chin upwards, and curled his fingers around the hilt of his sword, finding comfort in its warm touch.

The Invisitae cried in unison:

"*Vias nostras infinitam!*"

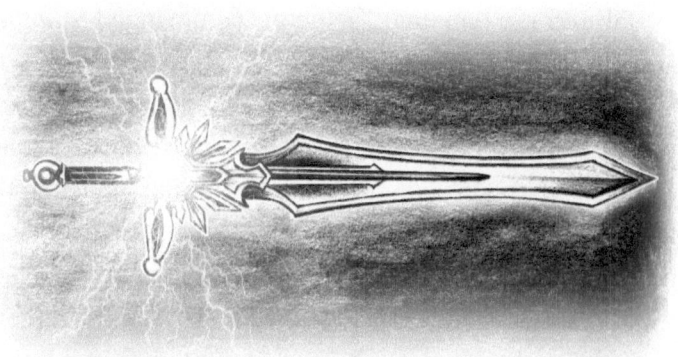

CHAPTER 27

ADARA FELT HER head swim at the weightless sensation accompanying teleportation. She landed heavily and gracelessly, knocking her knees against the smooth marble floor. She tried to arrest her fall with her palms, but they dangled uselessly behind her back and she heard the crunch of bone as her nose connected sharply against the stone floor.

"Take off the blindfold," someone commanded. *Another familiar voice*, Adara thought. *Were there no limits to treachery?*

Adara felt the scratch of the cloth against her hypersensitive skin, and opened her eyes. Before her stood Zachariah, accompanied with four others decked in steel masks of animal aspect. She recognised the twins who had helped capture her by their feline masks. Between them stood the snakelike man who had captured her in the first place, his face nearly split into two by an eerie smile. And directly in her line of sight stood a slender man who seemed to eclipse those around him. His dark hair shone against the steel of his mask. The mask he wore was simple, and did little to cover his angular features, his full lips, and his piercing golden eyes. Adara felt faint, as if the air had been forcibly ejected from her lungs.

"Hello, Adara!" Surazal called out. "I'm glad to finally meet you, as I am."

Adara tried to mask her shock, but failed to stop her eyebrows from rising to meet her hairline.

"Are you surprised?" Lazarus said, sounding amused.

Adara conveyed what she had to by spitting at his feet. He stepped back, laughing heartily.

"I've always liked your spunk. That's what makes you such an exceptional warrior, Bellator," he said, almost fondly.

"But that's not why I need you," he went on, stepping closer and beckoning the male twin forward with a swish of his fingers. The man covered the distance in two strides, pulling Adara to her feet and holding her back to prevent her from assaulting Lazarus. "You have some information that belongs to me. And I fully intend to extract it from you, by any means possible." His tone remained matter-of-fact throughout, chilling Adara more than any amount of threats he could have thrown her way.

"So tell me, Adara. Where is the Fountain of tainted water?" he asked.

"What good will that information do you?" Adara asked.

"You see, Adara. I never asked to become an Invisitus. In my adolescence, I had an unfortunate run-in with a dead man's dagger. It seemed he had tried to Turn himself, and died in the process. But I was not so lucky." His face contorted with scorn.

"I refuse to live this way."

"What good will the Fountain do to you?" Adara asked, bewildered and more than a little frightened.

"You're a smart girl, and you're Sapiens's apprentice. Don't tell me you don't know what happens to an Invisitus if they ingest tainted water."

Realisation dawned on Adara. He needed the water to complete the formulation of the potion for the reversal of the Change. He would drink the Reversal Potion and it would be administered to the Invisitae secretly, perhaps by somehow poisoning their food and drink with it. And so Lazarus would risk the lives of all the Invisitae – including his own – to get his grimy hands on the final ingredient in his admittedly ingenious plan.

"Reversing a Change of that magnitude . . . you could kill us all!"

"Still a better fate than living as freaks of nature, a life in exile!" The silver in Lazarus's eyes gleamed.

"You're completely mad," Adara whispered, knowing full well that he was anything but. Lazarus was a dangerous breed, completely convinced that his actions played towards the greater good. His fanaticism made him a formidable opponent; he wasn't insane, just completely lost to his cause.

"It would be in your best interests to answer my question, Adara. I'd hate to spill innocent blood. It does create a fearful mess," he said, polishing his metal knuckle brace on his cloak.

Adara stared steadfastly at Lazarus.

"I would rather die,"she said.

Without looking up from his brace he countered,

"That can also be arranged. Though keep in mind, *Bellator*, that losing you will mean we can destroy the Invisitae. One. At. A. Time."

Adara's mind raced, desperately trying to devise a way to escape. She was running out of time, and her limited choice of mediocre options made her choice all the more difficult.

"You're a smart girl, I trust you'll make the right decision," Surazal said.

He was right; she was smart. And so she knew when it was time to give up, and when to keep fighting. Zachariah was wrong, she was an *incredible* actress.

Her time in the spotlight had arrived.

Adara's breathing grew shallow, and her gaze grew unfocused. She teetered around on unsteady legs before falling heavily onto the masked twin. She panted and scrabbled weakly at his leg with her bound wrists. He stepped back, flabbergasted, and she swiped the knife sheathed in his boot, undetected. She crumpled to the floor, as though she had fainted, and flopped on the ground so her hands behind her back were concealed from them.

"What's gotten into her?" Lazarus asked Zachariah. "Did you hurt her?"

Zachariah hastily sputtered his denial:

"It must be the prolonged exposure to steel. It's weakened her body."

Adara lay facing the group, and began frantically sawing at the steel circlet round her wrists. The metal was pliant, and the knife sharp, so she made quick work of sawing through the band.

She heard Lazarus bark orders at the snakelike man and the other Invisitus to help the man carry her out of the room to get some fresh air.

She took care to remain a limp deadweight, and hold the two halves of her circlet in place, as not to signal that anything was amiss.

The trio carried her out in haste. The moment the tang of sea salt reached her nostrils, she felt invigorated. Zachariah was right; she *had* been weakened by her time in the steel cell. She felt the exhaustion melt away, and her headache receded to a dull throb. She scoped out the area mentally, realising that she was a few feet from the edge of the cliff she'd seen in her vision.

"Put her down!" Lazarus ordered, and his companions complied.

"Now, she can—"

Adara sprang up before she could finish, and knocked the heads of the surprised serpentine man and the other male assassin together. The clang of metal made Lazarus turn to face her, his features growing mildly annoyed.

"I really thought you were smarter than that." He shook his head, as if genuinely disappointed with her. But Adara didn't care. She was finally free. She was—

An invisible blow to the solar plexus winded Adara, and she fell forward, choking. Something else yanked her upright once again by her hair, and she felt a cold ridge of metal press into her throat. Belatedly, she recognised it as the metal knuckle brace she'd seen Lazarus sporting.

"Foolish child," Lazarus crooned in her ear, "you should know better than to challenge your teacher in a fight."

She cringed away from his warm breath on her neck. He turned his back to the sea, and addressed Zachariah.

"Finish her."

"The greatest honour you have entrusted me with, Master." Zachariah grinned like a puppy given a treat.

Adara clawed helplessly at the knuckle brace, succeeding only in shredding the skin of her fingers on its serrated surface. She felt the stares of the three assassins and Zachariah on her, and realised that struggle was futile. She'd done all she could, but it hadn't been enough.

At least the secret is safe, she thought as Zachariah advanced towards her, knife drawn. At least she hadn't doomed her whole race. After all, what was the value of one life weighed against so, so many?

Zachariah smirked as he raised the knife above his head, ready to strike. The gleam in his eyes showed how much he had waited for this moment, to destroy the little child who made his powers seem trivial in comparison, the girl who'd won over his own mentor's heart, and doomed him to a lifetime of being second choice. She saw no remorse in his eyes, nor did she expect to see any.

She closed her eyes. She couldn't bear to see the knife slashing through the air before it slashed through her. She felt Lazarus's brace break the skin of her throat and draw blood, and felt a pang of fear, accompanied with a thought for the boy she'd left behind, the only other person with the burden she carried.

I didn't even get to say goodbye to him.

She heard the telltale sign of the knife swishing through the air, and in her panic her eyes flew open of their own volition. She didn't want to die, she didn't want to go like this. She squirmed and kicked, watching the sunlight glint off the sharpened blade as it slashed towards her chest . . .

CHAPTER 28

AND STOPPED, MILLIMETRES away from the fabric of her tunic. Zachariah looked confused, and Adara heard the rumble of Lazarus's voice over the sound of blood rushing through her ears.

"What on earth is the meaning of this?" he shouted, urging Zachariah to continue. But instead, the man jerked his arm to the side, flinging the knife off the edge of the cliff and into the sea.

His confusion turned to pain, and he gripped the edges of his mask as he sank to the ground, rocking back and forth.

"Stand up, Zachariah! I command you to stand up!" Lazarus's brace pressed deeper into her sternum, and she choked.

Zachariah began rocking back and forth and keening, as if struck with intolerable pain. Adara watched as thick vines sprouted out from the ground around him and wrapped themselves around his limbs like predatory snakes, the man powerless to stop it.

Adara felt Lazarus's indecision: should he help his friend, or keep hold of her?

Zachariah continued the terrible keening noise, writhing on the ground as the vines wrapped themselves thickly around his middle. She had never seen anything like it.

A sound like splintering glass followed by a series of thuds filled the air. Adara watched as a group of ten Invisitae dressed in battle armour materialised in front of her. The warrior Invisitae teleported up to the human assassins and engaged them in heated battle. The remaining two, slightly older and more weathered than the rest, stayed put. Adara saw the silver sheen covering their eyes, and realised that they were responsible for Zachariah's sudden collapse.

"But he was wearing his mask! How could Sapiens control his mind through that?"Lazarus's disbelief was palpable.

"Don't underestimate the old man," Adara managed to choke out. Lazarus gritted his teeth, and dug his knuckles deeper into Adara's throat. Rivulets of blood trickled down her front, and she gasped in pain.

Suddenly, the periwinkle blue of the sky turned to the inky black of the night, and a torrential downpour started, accelerating the growth of the vines. Adara heard the confused cries of the assassins, and felt Lazarus stiffen behind her.

She tilted her face towards the sky and scanned it for his familiar face. She knew he would save her, her brilliant teammate. He always would.

A flash of lightning hit the ground directly in front of Lazarus, and he jumped back, dragging Adara with him. She watched as a figure descended through the skies. She could only see the glint of his dark hair and the gleaming silver of his eyes, but that was enough to recognise him.

"Let her go," Elijah boomed, the wind surrounding him amplifying his words. He brandished his gleaming sword, the flashes of white-hot lightning in the sky reflected in its polished blade. *Where did he get that sword?*Adara thought.

Adara felt Lazarus's chest rumble as he laughed. He withdrew the hand around her neck, and she heard the grating of metal against metal as he drew out a knife and placed it where his hand was.

Elijah had been about to take a step forward, but he stopped mid-step as Lazarus hissed,

"Come any closer, and I rip her head off."

Elijah considered his options: he couldn't strike Lazarus with lightning while he was still in contact with Adara; he couldn't attack at all, with the knife held to his friend's throat. Her eyes pleaded with him to attack, to do *something*. But he couldn't risk it.

"There's a good fellow. You could learn something from your friend, Adara. He's very obedient," he said, tapping her chin with the flat of his blade.

"Speaking of obedience, Elijah, tell your friend over here to tell me where the Fountain is, or I'll gut her like a pig," he said through gritted teeth.

"He will do no such thing," Sapiens rumbled, stepping in front Elijah and placing a hand in front of him as if to shield him. "Unhand the girl, Lazarus."

Lazarus shrugged, a graceful movement that stirred his entire body.

"So be it."

Lazarus raised his dagger, poised to plunge it directly into her trachea. The sounds of fighting behind Elijah faded into the distance, as if he'd encased himself within a bubble. Time slowed down. Elijah tried to jump past Sapiens's hand, but the older man held onto his armour, unyielding.

Sapiens's eyes flashed, and he raised his free hand towards Lazarus. Lazarus's eyes widened fractionally behind his mask, and he worried his lip as he fought against Sapiens's influence.

"I told you not to underestimate him," Adara said, her voice quavering unsteadily.

Sapiens flicked his wrist, and Lazarus hissed in pain as he tried to work against his body's movements. Elijah increased the intensity of the rain above Lazarus with a swipe of his sword and commanded the wind to buffet his hand. The man sputtered under the sudden downpour, but he didn't lose his concentration. His hand quivered as he fought against Sapiens, and his other hand tightened around Adara's waist, making her cry out in pain.

Sapiens gritted his teeth at Lazarus's resistance. It must have been difficult to control his mind through the steel mask, Elijah thought. He marvelled at the strength and skill Sapiens possessed. Sweat poured down the old man's forehead, and he began panting with exhaustion. He couldn't keep this up much longer.

Elijah heard an impassioned cry behind him, and he whirled around, sword raised. His sword clashed against the lance held by the fair-haired assassin Elijah recognised as one of Adara's abductors. Elijah bellowed a cry and lunged at the man, and slashed at his chest. The man blocked the strike by a hair's breadth and swerved to the side, slashing out with his lance and catching Elijah on the hip with the blunt body of the weapon.

Elijah roared and slashed out again, laying a blow on the man's weapon shoulder. The man stepped back with the force of the blow, and Elijah swerved behind the man and struck at the back of his knees. The man fell to the ground, a silent scream playing upon his lips.

Elijah straightened and kicked the assassin's weapon out of his reach. He looked towards the warrior Invisitae, seeing them surrounding the two assassins, who stood with their backs to each other. Despite their numbers, the warriors couldn't keep up with the unorthodox style of fighting the two favoured. The two worked in unison, a deadly blur of whirling limbs and slashing weapons.

Elijah trained his eyes on the duo, and raised Tempest to the sky. A bolt of white lightning arced down from the sky and hit the tip of Elijah's sword. He swerved his sword and jabbed it in the direction of the assassins, sending the bolt of lightning flying towards them. The lightning branched into two forks, each hitting the assassins square in the chest. They cried out in unison and flew backwards in the air, skidding in the wet mud before landing by the steel building.

A cry of unadulterated pain rang out behind Elijah, and he turned to see Sapiens crumple to the ground in a heap, a savage light in Lazarus's eyes.

"No!" Lucian and Adara's collective screams tore through the rain, and he materialised near Sapiens's prone body. Elijah ran to his side, to see the hilt of a dagger protruding from his chest. Crimson blood pooled under the old man, and his skin was rapidly turning sallow. His breaths turned shallow and rapid, and he began coughing blood. Lucian grabbed Sapiens's arm and teleported him under the shade of the steel building, out of the rain.

"You were foolish to underestimate me," Lazarus rasped, and Elijah gritted his teeth.

Elijah saw red, and his eyes turned silver. His blood thrummed with rage as he raised his sword and propelled himself towards Lazarus and Adara using a tailwind.

Lazarus smiled wickedly.

"Wrong move," he whispered.

Elijah stopped his sword in mid-swing, and Lazarus turned sharply, flinging Adara away from his body. The girl gasped as she teetered on the edge of the cliff, desperately trying to steady herself. But Lazarus's thrust was too strong.

Adara's scream was lost in the sound of the shrieking wind as she fell towards the ravenous waves.

CHAPTER 29

Time.

Stood.

Still.

CHAPTER 30

A STRANGLED CRY ripped itself from Elijah, and he lunged towards Adara, missing her by a hair's breadth. Elijah fell to his knees, stretching a hand out over the edge of the cliffinspite of the futility of the action.

The sounds around him coalesced into a horrifying cacophony which made his head throb. The tendons in his neck went taut as he screamed, blood rushing to his face and colouring it.

His nightmare had come true.

The primal thrum of power pervaded his senses, drowning out the sounds of the thunderous storm and the lamenting wind. This time, Elijah didn't protest when his irises disappeared behind a sheen of opaque silver. It didn't block his vision, he found; it enhanced it, helping him see distances farther than normal. He peered over the edge, catching a glimpse of Adara's red hair flailing, metres above the rising crests of the waves crashing on the rocks at the foot of the cliff,and dropping swiftly. He joined his palms and scrunched his eyes closed, tears leaving tracks on his cheeks as he concentrated.

*

The wind whistled by Adara as she fell, tugging at her hair like a petulant child and grabbing fistfuls of her clothes, as if trying to stop her from falling to her watery grave. Her mouth formed a perfect "o", but she couldn't hear herself scream over the ire of the wind.

The stomach-dropping feeling she'd felt at the edge of the cliff had only intensified as she'd continued her descent. Adara had given up flailing her arms and legs, realising the futility of it. *Even you can't fight gravity*, she thought, *nobody can.* With her powers weakened, she was like any human.

But Elijah had done it repeatedly, hadn't he?

Adara recalled the awe she'd felt the first time he'd demonstrated his affinity, the euphoria she'd felt at having such a strong ally – such a strong partner. They were two of a kind, her and Elijah. They would have done great things together.

Adara!

Adara started at the sound of the familiar voice, until she realised that it was inside her head. Somewhere along the line, her fear must have stripped away the wards in her mind.

And she realised that stomach-lurching sense of freefall was gone. She was falling, but slower, the winds that roiled about her were indeed fighting gravity. Or maybe a vestige of her own powers was returning . . .

Adara, hold on! Hold on for just—

Elijah broke off in mid-thought, and Adara felt a pang of fear. What exactly happened to him just then? But she couldn't help quell the palpitations in her heart. He was going to save her. She knew he would.

She felt the spray on her back, and closed her eyes, praying he wasn't too late.

*

Elijah had been in deep concentration, when Lazarus grabbed him by the scruff of his neck and hauled him to his feet roughly. Elijah howled and thrashed, clawing at the muscled arm squeezing his waist in a vice like grip. He was so close, he couldn't give up now.

Lazarus laughed at his animalistic desperation.

"She's gone now, there's no point screaming," he crooned.

Elijah's blood surged in his veins, responding to his climbing urgency and anger. Electricity thrummed beneath his skin, making it itch maddeningly, as if begging for release. Lazarus's arms tightened around Elijah, and his powers surged at the pressure his enemy's arms exerted on his hypersensitive skin.

Lazarus leaned into Elijah's ear, his hot breath scalding Elijah's tingling skin, making it scream in agony. He whispered,

"You failed, Stormbringer."

You failed, Stormbringer.

The powers in Elijah erupted from his skin like a tidal wave, crashing over his head and engulfing him in a fiery orb of light. Lazarus jumped back from the boy screaming incoherently, as the unadulterated energy singed his flesh. The bright blue light engulfed Elijah from his view, and Lazarus shielded his burning retinas with his scorched arms. He scuttled away desperately from the blazing orb and tripped over the supine form of the unconscious Zachariah, still bound in Lucian's vines. He fell to the ground with a strangled cry, the image of the lightning scorched into the backs of his eyelids.

Elijah roared, and the sphere of blue light expanded into a column of light that shot up into the heavens, incinerating the storm clouds and evaporating the rain in their way, a circle of pure light in the darkness of the raging sky.

*

The spray on Adara's back began to thicken, and the acrid smell of salt burned her nostrils. Her heart bleated in panic. The inevitability of death struck her like a sledgehammer, and the zooming of pale sky and sea spray seemed to slow down. The very wind seemed to caress her shoulders and back, as if cushioning her fall. Jets of wind and spray touched her back with a feather-like gentleness, and seemed as if they were arresting her fall. Perhaps this wasn't such a bad way to go, after all.

Adara took a few moments to realise that she had indeed stopped falling and been suspended in mid-air. Her heart leaped and sang with joy, tears streaming past her eyes and into her hair.

Suddenly, she saw a blinding column of blue light emanate from the top of the cliff, reaching skyward. The light washed over her skin in deliciously warm waves, and she realised that Elijah was the cause.

Suddenly, she felt the wind beneath her grow in fervour, stirring her hair impatiently as it pushed her upright. Adara felt the cool caress of the sea breeze on her face, and felt the disappointed patter of sea spray on the bottoms of her scuffed shoes. Adara straightened herself unsteadily as the wind propelled her upwards, bringing her closer and closer to the lip of the cliff.

*

Elijah drew his hands into fists, and sauntered towards Lazarus, the crackling fingers of lightning scorching a trail into the grass beneath him.

He came to a stop over the cowering figure of Lazarus who shied away from the blinding light, and opened his mouth, as if to say something, when a sweet peal of laughter pierced the air.

Lazarus looked around blindly for the origin of the sound, but the intensity of the lightning blurred its surroundings into a watery nothingness. The cold grip of fear tightened around his heart.

"He didn't fail, Lazarus. *You did.*"

CHAPTER 31

LAZARUS'S BLOOD RAN cold at the feminine sound of the voice. It must have simply been his guilty conscience acting out on him. He'd always had a soft spot for Adara's free-spirited and carefree attitude, the way she shouldered such a burden from such a young age without so much as a whine.

You're not hallucinating, her voice spoke conspiratorially in his head, and he jumped at the sound, eliciting another laugh from her.

He shielded his eyes from the glowering boy and his shield of lightning, and spotted a hazy speck of red making its way in their general direction, growing larger and larger as it approached until it took on a human shape with fiery red curls, the toes of its boots skimming the tips of grass swaying in the strong breeze. The girl was wide-eyed, her pale skin a beacon in the darkness. In the bluish light, she looked ethereal, almost wraith-like. This was definitely a hallucination, if he'd ever had one.

Lazarus blinked rapidly and sputtered,

"But how . . .? I saw you fall . . ."

Elijah's silver eyes flashed brilliantly and his lip curled. He flicked his wrist, as if swatting at a particularly bothersome fly, and Lazarus found himself sailing through the air before colliding sharply with the muddy ground and skidding to a stop a few feet away. He wiped flecks of mud from his eyes and struggled to his feet, eyes trained warily on Elijah. Suddenly, the boy disappeared, and Lazarus was thrown into complete darkness at the sudden disappearance of the glare of the lightning. But the boy materialised a few feet from him, and sent a flash of lightning careening towards the man. Lazarus swerved out of the way, the lightning hitting him in the hip.

He sucked in a pained breath through his teeth and lunged at Elijah, tackling him around his waist and pinning him to the ground. Elijah hit the ground with enough force to knock the air out of his lungs, and retaliated by flinging Lazarus off his body with a concentrated blast of wind. Lazarus snarled, and pounced again.

Elijah had just gotten to his feet when he was hit square on the jaw. Before he could recover, Lazarus punched him in the stomach, leaving broken skin and bruises where the steel knuckle brace made contact. Elijah spat blood on the grass, and tried to scope out his opponent, but he couldn't see him. Elijah remembered the lightning-quick strikes Lazarus had dealt earlier on, before he'd discovered his true identity and realised that the man was using his affinity to best Elijah. Elijah withdrew his sword from his scabbard and willed the lightning in his body to flow into the cool metal.

Lazarus materialised inches from Elijah's right hand, and he struck out, cutting through only air as Lazarus spun out of range, teleporting to his other side and landing another blow on his jaw. Elijah roared in frustration as Lazarus landed three more blows in succession, while Elijah swung his sword aimlessly.

Anger makes him unstable, Elijah remembered Adara telling him, and he took a deep breath. She'd said it about Sebastian, but it applied to himself, too. Elijah closed his eyes, concentrating on the sound of the wind rushing past his ears, and the pulse of blood through his veins. He heard a shift to his right, and slashed his sword in a horizontal arc, to be rewarded with the sound of sizzling flesh and a strangled cry. He had caught Lazarus in his right thigh, and the man dropped to his knees, cradling the scorched wound and smoking cloth.

"This isn't over, Stormbringer!" Lazarus said through gritted teeth, spitting the last word at Elijah. Elijah breathed heavily, tired out from the exertion. The power in his veins sputtered, and the crackling around his sword flickered feebly before going out. The rain subsided, and the dark clouds dissipated with a wave of his hand, taking with them the darkness of the day. Elijah's fingers slackened with exhaustion, and the sword fell to the ground at his feet, but he paid no attention to it.

Elijah turned to face Adara, who still stood suspended over the ground, her crimson locks flowing around her shoulders and framing her face like a halo. His heart spasmed with relief at his friend's well-being, and he opened his mouth to tell her, when her eyes widened.

"Elijah, look out!"she screamed.

Time flowed like sluggish treacle around Elijah as he turned, only to come face to face with Lazarus lunging at him with Elijah'ssword in his hand. He remembered Lazarus saying, "Never turn your back to your opponent," and marvelled at how incredibly stupid he'd just been.

Elijah was blinded by panic, letting the blade within inches of his neck before he turned on his heel and vaulted away from Lazarus, coming to stand on Adara's side.

He panted with exhaustion and adrenaline and turned to face Adara, who stood with her arms stretched out towards Lazarus. Her face wore a look of utmost concentration, her eyes unwavering. Beads of sweat peppered her forehead like crystalline drops, and she worried her lip with concentration. Elijah followed her gaze, and stepped back in awe.

In front of him stood Lazarus frozen in mid-swing, a savagely malicious grin distorting his features. Elijah stared, unblinking, at the statue of his worst enemy.

"What did you do to him?"he asked.

"A time-binder illusion," answeredAdaraas she lowered her hands."This is a small trick Sapiens taught me, but I'm not allowed to use it unless it's life or death; playing with time never ends well.But it seems I'm getting my affinities back . . . I couldn't stop myself falling a while back." She smiled gratefully.

She held Elijah's rough hand in her own smooth ones, and teleported them to Lazarus's side. The man looked positively manic up close, a feral glint fracturing the silvery glints in his golden eyes. Elijah reached out and gently removed the sword from Lazarus's grasp, sure that the man would emerge from his stillness and chop his arm off. But the time binder held, and Elijah returned the sword to his scabbard without incident.

"This lasts for only a few minutes, so I have to be quick," Adara said, placing a palm on either side of Lazarus's face and gripping firmly. Elijah stiffened; He'd seen his mother twist the necks of the chickens they'd had on their farm, and she had done it in much the same manner. Surely she didn't mean to kill him . . .

Adara's eyes widened, and she burst out laughing. Elijah was taken aback. How could she laugh under so much pressure? She released Lazarus and turned to speak to Elijah.

"You really must learn to guard your thoughts, Elijah. You're practically shoving them into my face." She giggled at the flush creeping across his cheeks, and turned to face the still Lazarus.

"I'm only going to erase all of his memories associated with the Invisitae and the Occidierum."

"What good will that do? He's a killer!" Elijah argued. "A cold blooded, good-for-nothing—"

"Did you ever wish you had had a choice?" Adara interrupted. "A choice to become an Invisitus?"

Elijah thought for a moment before nodding the affirmative.

"You may have chosen the same path, who knows. But I'd imagine a choice would have helped things along nicely. I'd imagine that's the reason for his misguided deeds," she said, closing her eyes. A golden glow emanated from her palms, bathing her face in soft light. She placed her palms once again on Lazarus's cheeks.

"Sapiens says that there is no good and bad in a person, only what they choose to do with what they have. You took the Change as an opportunity, and Lazarus as a burden. Two sides of the same coin, if you will. This will put him out of his misery, and save us a headache."

The soft glow from her fingertips flowed into Lazarus's skin, lighting it with a healthy glow. Elijah watched Adara as she scrunched her nose and eyebrows, deep in concentration. Elijah watched, fascinated, as the murderous glare in Lazarus's eyes grew docile and unfocused. The hard lines and set of his jaw softened into an expression of calm, and his arms fell to his sides. A sigh of relief emanated from the man, as if a heavy weight had been lifted off his chest. Adara guided the body onto the grass, placing Lazarus's head down carefully and letting go, taking the golden glow with her. She joined her hands, and the light subsided.

"He should be out for a while," she said, standing up. She inconspicuously rubbed her eyes and sniffed before turning to Elijah and smiling. She took a step towards him and her knees buckled. Elijah ran forward, catching her in his arms and steadying her.

"Thank you," she said tiredly, but her smile shone bright.

"What for?" Elijah winked at her, placing an arm around her waist and helping her stand. She threw her arms around him, leaning heavily into his neck.

"For everything." Elijah blushed at the happy feeling blossoming in his chest, and hugged her back.

"Adara! Elijah! You must hurry!" They sprang apart at the unexpected appearance and urgency of the foreign voice. It was Sven, the boulder-like Invisitus who had helped save Elijah in the secret passage. Elijah's heart skipped a beat, afraid at the nature of his sudden appearance and the pained expression on his face.

"It's Sapiens. He's dying."

CHAPTER 32

ELIJAH AND ADARA thundered through the winding passageways, following Sven as he lead them to the medical chamber. Elijah recognised them from his first night in the Brotherhood's labyrinth.

"We're not allowed to teleport into the chamber? Just how badly hurt is he?" Adara asked, worry pouring into her words.

They burst into the room, which seemed to have shrunk in size from the last time Elijah had been here. It was full of warriors and Elders, who parted to allow the duo to approach Sapiens's bed.

Sapiens's papery-white skin blended into the pale bed-sheets, his normally sharp eyes milky but lucid as they scanned the room for something. His eyes stopped on the two children, and he raised a weak arm, beckoning them towards him with a long finger. The two approached warily,

Elijah shocked at his level of deterioration and Adara swallowing tears.

Lucian rose from Sapiens's side.

"He's been asking for the both of you, repeatedly," he said. "Said he couldn't leave your side at Castlemartin, that you needed him. But I couldn't have just . . .I couldn't have—" his voice broke mid-sentence, and he went to stand at Sapiens's head.

I am too weak to speak, my children. Sapiens's voice was feeble in Elijah's head, practically unrecognisable.

My time has come, and there is little I can do about it. A sob escaped from Adara's throat, and she fell at Sapiens's side, her body quivering with sobs as she reached out to take his hand.

My beautiful, beautiful Bellator, Sapiens said, stroking her hand with the pad of his thumb. *I have seen you grow from a wee babe to a beautiful, headstrong young woman. No man I have ever seen is a match for your strength and wit.* Adara smiled a watery smile, and Sapiens blinked gently. *You are nothing short of a daughter to me, and it is for that very reason that I expect great things from you.*

Elijah noticed the slight tremor in his hands, the papery sound of Sapiens swallowing. He noticed a slight discolouration of the sheets bundled around Sapiens and noticed that they were stained with flecks of black and red. *The knife was poisoned,* Elijah thought.

You are correct, Elijah. Despite Lucian's valiant efforts, this particular injury could not be fixed. Sapiens coughed slightly, wincing as his body shook.

I can hardly articulate the pride I feel, Elijah. The rate at which you have grown and improved is incomparable. You have accomplished so much all on your own – the only reason I despair is that I won't get to see you grow further. Despite himself, Elijah felt a wetness stain his cheeks.

I wish I could have spent more time with you, to help you discover the hidden depths of your potential. And, of course, answer your limitless questions. Elijah cracked a rueful smile at this, and Sapiens chuckled. Suddenly, his chuckle evolved into a full-blown cough which wracked his body and made the veins in his neck bulge with exertion. He brought up a hand over his mouth. He choked wetly, and spots of red appeared on his palm. Lucian jumped to help Sapiens, but he waved him away adamantly, settling back on his pillows. Lucian bent and gently wiped his lips and palm with a small towel.

Adara and Elijah, you are the hope of our people. You have proven your strength and capabilities and defeated a fearsome enemy of the Invisitae, but there are many more out there – it is a burden the Different have to bear. He winced as he turned to face the two. *Together you must lead the Brotherhood into a new era of prosperity in my absence. I am certain you will accomplish great deeds together.*

Sapiens extended his other hand to Elijah, and he took it. His hand was frigid and smooth like marble, as if death had already wrapped its unfeeling fingers around the old man. A single tear ran down Sapiens's hollow cheeks and made a wet spot on his pillow. He tried to smile, and struggled to stop it from appearing as a grimace. Elijah's heart broke, watching this man that always had a smile on his face struggle to summon one. Adara sniffled and bit her lip, struggling not to cry. Elijah remembered the vision she had showed him, and his lip quivered. Who would she have left in the world, after Sapiens passed?

Sapiens coughed once, and his grip tightened on Elijah's fingers. Elijah looked away from his hands and into his face. His eyes spoke volumes as he said, *I want to see your light one last time before I go.*

Elijah extracted his hands from Sapiens's and joined his palms, as if in prayer. Within seconds, a soft orb of blue light was cupped in his hands. Sapiens reached towards the light, wonder written across his features.

He opened his mouth, his lips quivering as he tried to form words. His gaze locked on the orb of lightning, he wheezed,

"You hold the sun in your palms."

He didn't speak again.

CHAPTER 33

"ADARA?"

Elijah shook her shoulder gently, and she woke with a start. She hadn't moved from her seat next to Sapiens's bed, desperately clutching onto his arm as if it were a lifeline, as if she was the one on the brink of death.

The day's events came crashing down on her, and her shoulders sagged with exhaustion. She pried her fingers from Sapiens's rapidly cooling ones, and turned to face Elijah. She saw the pained expression on his face, and knew that he was thinking of the vision she had shown him. She was about to spit a retort at him; she disliked pity more than she disliked losing, and woe betide anyone who pitied her, for they would surely incur her wrath. But one look at his sorrowful eyes showed her that he did not pity her, but instead he felt her pain.

Instantly her face crumpled, and she fell into his arms, her body heaving with gut-wrenching sobs. She leaned heavily on him and her nails dug into his shoulder, but he didn't complain. He held her as she cried, and held her for a long time after her tears subsided.

*

After what seemed like hours, Lucian sent Matron to call the two to Sapiens's room. Elijah half-expected the qualities that were so completely Sapiens to have disappeared with their owner, but the room felt the same as ever; the tottering piles of books, the musty smell of old paper and the large, ornate desk – they all remained. Somehow, Elijah felt at peace in the room, as if Sapiens's spirit lingered there.

They walked past a stack of storybooks and stood face-to-face with the circle of Elders, Lucian standing in his place next to the empty space where the Eldest had once stood.

Lucian closed his eyes briefly and opened them again, and spoke.

"Today has been a day of great triumph and great sorrow for the Brotherhood. We defeated our fearsome enemies, Lazarus and the Occidierum, in an epic battle of which our Stormbringer and Bellator were the heroes. However, we have also lost an integral member of our Brotherhood and the Invisitus community, Eldest Sapiens." Everyone in the room bowed their heads in silence.

"It is no doubt a devastatingly distressing event, but Sapiens would not have wanted us to spend our time mourning him. Sapiens lived a long and fulfilling life, guiding the Invisitae in their quest to make the world a safer place for its inhabitants. But more than that, he was an exceptional leader, friend, teacher and father." He looked towards the sniffling Adara at the last word.

"Stormbringer, Elijah. Please step forward," Lucian called. Adara squeezed his fingers, and he went and stood in front of the Elders.

"Due to a series of unfortunate events, you are being found without a master to guide and nurture you on your journey to uncovering your full potential as an Invisitus. Consequently, the Elders have determined that you be assigned to me as my new apprentice."

Elijah nodded and smiled softly, noting the encouraging smile on Lucian's face, despite everything.

"You may take your place." Elijah obeyed.

"Bellator, Adara. Please step forth."

Adara took the place Elijah had vacated seconds ago, and stood straight in front of the Elders, her chin held high.

Brother Lucian cleared his throat and said,

"Before he passed on, Eldest Sapiens made one wish of his heard loud and clear: that Adara, his apprentice, be instated in his stead as the Eldest of the Brotherhood."

Adara's violet eyes bugged and she stood agape, her mouth opening and closing like a fish's. The sudden loss of composure would have been comical if not for the audible thrum of her power in the air.

"Considering that you are far from having completed your training, however, the Elders and I have had to make a slight concession."

He paused, and indicated for someone behind him to step forward. Two men strode out from behind Lucian, one supporting the other, who leaned heavily on his shoulder. However, their faces remained obscured by the shadow of a tower of books.

"At the eve of your training you were assigned not one, but two mentors, so that your training would not be disrupted in an event such as this.

"Therefore, Bellator, you will take your position as the Eldest of the Brotherhood. However, you will be assisted in your duties by you mentor, Brother Fabian."

At this, Fabian walked out of the shadows, heavily supported by a grinning Sebastian. Elijah's eyes widened. Fabian looked slightly bruised and he had a limp, but he had still managed to heal at a remarkable pace. Jarrod and Marian had truly done an excellent job.

Fabian disentangled his arm from Sebastian's shoulder, and opened them wide. Adara ran into his arms with an exuberant squeal, and he winced at the impact but held on fast. Tears of relief mingled with sadness poured down his face, but he wiped them and smiled blearily at Adara.

Elijah shifted uncomfortably at the display of affection, and began focusing on the frayed threads in his breeches. Someone cleared his throat and Elijah looked up, his eyes meeting Fabian's piercing green ones. Fabian stared at the boy for a long time, before extending an arm to him too.

Elijah tried to hide his beam as he rushed into the embrace.

EPILOGUE

MARIAN SAT ON the edge of the bed, holding in her hands her son's shirt, the only one she had dared keep. She sniffled into the fabric, hoping the young boy tidying the room couldn't hear her. Jarrod, for his part, tactfully ignored Marian's soft snuffles.

She had no idea what had happened to her boy; he had a delicate constitution, like his father. But surely he had enough of her in him to be able to hold his own in a fight. It had been better with Fabian around. At least she'd had someone to fuss over and take care of. The sweet, open smiles he frequently threw her way also helped keep her mind off the danger her son was inevitably in. She wrung her hands, her brow crinkling with worry.

Jarrod stopped by the window, looking out at the heat wavesshimmering over the baked earth. When Elijah had described a farm to him, this was not what he'd had in mind. The place was a wasteland. In the past several hours, every plant he had succeeded in growing had turned to brittle dust in no time. This place needed water, and tons of it.

As soon as he formed that thought, a clap of thunder sounded in the air – a sound so seemingly out of place in the dry countryside that Jarrod involuntarily took a step back. He looked towards Marian to see if he had imagined the sound, or if she had heard it too. But she was lost deep in her thoughts, so Jarrod turned his attention back to the window.

As he watched, the blinding blue of the sky turned murky and dark with the presence of cumulonimbus clouds. The clouds spread as far as the eye could see and hung low on the horizon. Three people materialised outside the house – Adara, Fabian and Sebastian. Jarrod stared in delight and teleported outside to greet them.

"We should go inside, Fabian," Sebastian suggested. Storms and the sick did not mix well. Fabian complied, and the two disappeared into the house, to be welcomed by Marion.

"Do you want to join them?" Jarrod asked Adara, knowing full well from the impish smile she gave him what her answer would be.

A second boom of thunder resounded, and Jarrod saw Marian jump with a start. She rushed to the window and peered out quizzically, her jaw unhinging at the presence of rain clouds. Jarrod saw her mouth move in excitement – no doubt she was talking about the unexpectedness of the storm.

Jarrod looked far up into the sky for his friend, and found him suspended in the middle of a sphere of wind. He screamed and waved his arms to get Elijah's attention, and the boy in the sky turned his silvered eyes towards Jarrod and smiled, returning the enthusiastic waves. Then, he raised his arms to the heavens, and the sky opened up.

Rain, deliciously cool rain fell to the dry ground, the impact of each raindrop sending plumes of dust into the air. The rain thickened into sheets, and the plumes of dust soon turned to squelches of mud. Adara squealed in excitement, and began prancing around the farmland, getting her clothes irrevocably dirty in the process.

Jarrod stretched his arms before him, palms facing downward. He felt a familiar tug in his gut, an almost primal response to the roaring of the elements, and thick green grass sprouted from the mud. Jarrod spread his fingers, thinking of as many different species of plants he could, painting the ground green.

*

Marian watched the scene from the bedroom window, her mouth falling open with awe. That miraculous healer could grow plants out of nothing. Healthy, vibrant hydrangeas and morning glory and foxgloves; ripe tomatoes and cabbages and carrots and juicy beets sprang up wherever he directed his silvery gaze. Fields of green corn stretched out to the horizon, trees burst into leaf and blossom.

Marian ran through the kitchen, flinging open the door to the house and joined the beautiful red-haired girl in her pirouetting around the now lush farmland. The vigorous rain made her feel rejuvenated, as if she'd aged backwards. She threw her hands up into the air and whirled over and over before collapsing on the lush, loamy soil. She threw her face up to the sky, catching the delicious elixir on her tongue.

If only Eli was here to see this, he'd be so happy! He's always loved the rains, Marian thought wistfully, twisting her sodden hair out of her face.

The girl stopped dancing and looked towards Marian. She smiled cheekily and said, "Look up!" before continuing her merry jig.

Marian looked up, not understanding the true purpose of the exercise. The rain fell in giant pellets, obscuring her vision. She shielded her eyes and peered back into the sky, and drew in a sharp breath.

Suspended above her head was Elijah. He was taller and more muscular than she remembered, but a mother never forgets. Eli had come back to see her.

She stood up and cupped her hands around her mouth.

"Eli!" she screamed into the sky, "Elijah! You come down here this instant!"

The boy looked to her with silvered eyes and beamed before beginning his descent. He hovered two feet over the ground before Marian snatched him out of the air and held him tightly to her. He laughed at her excitement, and she beamed and started laughing too. The two sank to the ground in a tangle of limbs, smiling and laughing so hard that they could no longer tell which were tears and which the rain.

*

And it just so happened that the farmer, just a few kilometres away, looked towards his neighbour's fields at the time that the clouds broke. He raised his dusty hands to the sky in wonder, letting the glistening drops caress his leathery skin. And if he saw a boy descend from the lap of the sky into his mother's arms, and saw a girl whirling faster and faster with every volley of rain, and saw a boy charm flora out of the ground, one will never know.

And if, when they were walking into the house, he saw the boy holding a piece of the sun in his hands, he kept his silence.

***

ACKNOWLEDGEMENTS

AS A SARCASTIC and (debatably) witty teenager, I often find myself scoffing at the phrase, "this book would not have been possible without (insert an army of names here)", but it is only years and multiple abandoned manuscripts later that I can fully appreciate the massive effort it takes to create a book. After all, stringing 26 letters into a sentence is only the beginning.

Before all else, I'd like to thank my mother. It's rarely easy to deal with a teenager, and even less feasible to manage a teenager with an overactive imagination and the words to express her mind's wanderings. I am in no way a patient person, but you are, and for that I am infinitely grateful.

Daddy, you always put off reading my book by telling me to "show it to Papa when it's finished", but you never hesitated to sit with me and talk me out of my frequent disillusionment with the book. You taught me what it meant to be committed, and that is the sole reason this story exists today.

Thanks to my sister for staying up late every night in order to learn what Elijah has been up to, and help guide me when I needed it the most. Thanks especially for the late night YouTube breaks, and even the cross-oceanic dance parties over Skype when the stress of work and writing got overwhelming.

Thanks to my grandparents for letting me be privy to your wonderful stories and encouraging me to create my own. Especially to Jejebapa, who said "the best storytellers are those with wandering minds – they never know where they'll end up and who they'll meet."

Thanks to my friends for their undying love and support, for illustrating my characters before even I knew what they looked like, and for constantly clamouring for more chapters. You kept me sane when everything got overwhelming, with your fun quips and fresh insights, and I love you all for that.

Avinash and Madan, your illustration for the cover is what made me truly believe that my story was real, and that it could be shared with the rest of the world. You never cease to amaze me.

A special thanks to the team at Crossword, and my team at WordIt. Rinky, Padmini and Malini – you are the holy trinity as far as I'm concerned. Publication is an alien land that even most adult writers have trouble navigating, so thank you for your constant guidance and support.

Thanks to my insane puppy for waking me up with his sporadic nightly barking when I stayed up too late writing and inevitably fell asleep (every time.) Thanks to Julie and Pushpa for making me endless cups of coffee, and listening to my constant whining during writer's block. Thanks to the books lining my shelves for helping me escape and find myself in so many different ways every time I turned the page.

And thank *you*, reader, for having the valour to stand alongside Elijah through his journey, and especially for sitting through this long and boring acknowledgement. (Seriously, how did you manage that??)

ABOUT THE AUTHOR

FROM THE MOMENT she could read, sixteen-year-old Archita Mishra has spent most of her life with her nose buried in a book, and only resurfaces when she is in need of another one. With such an insatiable appetite for knowledge, it is no surprise that she spends most of her waking time creating worlds, painting and weaving stories.

She could spin tales out of nothing and her audience (primarily her mother and unassuming older sister) was often left questioning the reality of her stories. Her fables were so well crafted and believable that as a toddler, she managed to convince a friend that she owned a massive dog, despite having the friend visit and find none. At the age of four, Archita penned (*read: scratched*) and illustrated (*read: scribbled*) her first novel *The Adventures of Animal X* and from that day forward, she had found her calling. Archita honed her writing skills throughout her years in the J.B. Petit High School for Girls, and although her artistic skills remained frozen in time, her writing flourished. A series of short stories, a few abandoned (*read: dormant*) ideas and a handful of poems later, Archita began conceptualising and writing her first official novel, *The Stormbringer*.

When Archita isn't seen reading or writing, she's often heard belting out lyrics of the latest Panic! at the Disco song, dancing – from classical Odissi to KPOP (she is the epitome of versatility, I'm sure you can tell), entertaining walkers at the local park with her powerhouse vocals, engaging in MUNs and carrying out student council activities at the Dhirubhai Ambani International School.

www.ingramcontent.com/pod-product-compliance
Lightning Source LLC
Chambersburg PA
CBHW030424180626
46812CB00005B/2165